MW00938227

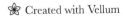 Created with Vellum

FORBIDDEN
Kiss

KELLI CALLAHAN

Chapter One

TAYLOR

"*H*ow does my dress look?" I turned around to check myself in the mirror and adjusted a couple of wrinkles in the fabric.

"It looks fine." My younger sister, Anna, looked up from her book for a moment and shrugged. "Why do you care anyway? It's not like you're going to buy anything."

"I want to blend in with the crowd—the best way to do that is to look like I belong there." My shoulders slumped forward, and I sighed.

I totally don't look like I belong there.

There was an art auction—technically, it was just a preview show for the art that was going to be auctioned so potential bidders could figure out what they wanted to bid on before the actual auction took place. Every year, Wellington's gave a few tickets to the art department at Carson Cove University so that a few students could come to the art show. It was a once in a lifetime opportunity for most students because very few of us were ever going to have the kind of wealth required to get a *real* invitation.

I didn't expect to actually win when I entered my name in

the raffle, but luck was on my side—the fact that I bought twenty raffle tickets might have had something to do with it too. It was my senior year of college, and my last chance to attend the art show, so I decided to take a risk. Thankfully, it paid off.

"Have you seen my crimson-sin lipstick?" I picked up my makeup bag and started digging through it.

"Why would you ask me?" Anna looked up from her book again. "If anyone in this house is borrowing your lipstick, it's not me. Mom was talking about lipstick a few days ago when she was getting ready for her date with Brad—or was it, Steve?"

"Right…" I nodded and made a beeline for my mother's bedroom.

Anna would rather die than wear lipstick.

My mom had been raiding my makeup since she decided that it was time to start dating again. I couldn't say much—I did the same thing to her when I first started wearing it. I still hadn't adjusted to the fact that my mom was going on dates with someone other than my dad, but he was the one that left, so I couldn't say much about it. At least someone in the house was getting some action. I was too busy with school to have a boyfriend, and Anna was technically old enough to start dating if she wanted to, but she always had her nose in a book. I'm wasn't sure she would even notice if a guy hit on her.

"Ah, there it is." I found my crimson-sin lipstick sitting on my mother's vanity—it was a stark contrast to the boring shades she usually wore.

Anna didn't look up at me when I walked back into my bedroom and started applying my lipstick. I had no idea why she even bothered to hang out in my room anymore—it used to our tradition after school every day, but it had been a long time since we shared any common interests. Our age difference had a lot to do with it. She was barely sixteen, and I was

2

twenty-three. I hated that we had drifted apart, but our lives were in different places. I was focused on graduating, finding a real job, and getting my own place. She was trying to survive high school, and if there was anything else going on, she didn't talk to me about it. The divorce seemed to impact her more than it did me. I was old enough to realize that the relationship was broken before our dad left, but she was still young and naive.

"Alright, I don't know when I'll be back—don't wait up." I tried some humor to see if I could get a smile out of my little sister.

"I never do." She looked up and rolled her eyes—but there was no smile.

Oh well, I tried...

The art show was being held at Wellington's Museum downtown, which was about thirty minutes away from my house. I waited for my phone to connect to the car so I would have some music for my drive and skipped over a couple of Ariana Grande songs so that I could listen to my latest jam, *Old Town Road* by Lil Nas X. I started singing along as I drove through the streets of the Mandalay Subdivision. I didn't live in the richest part of Carson Cove by any means, but my neighborhood was picture-perfect suburbia with well-manicured lawns and flower beds everywhere.

I always thought I would leave Carson Cove behind when it was time for me to go to college, but money got tight after my parents divorced. Living at home and attending Carson Cove University was the best option for everyone—I certainly didn't want to drown myself in student loans and work two jobs on top of going to school.

Getting a chance to go to the art show is a definite perk of staying behind—I wouldn't have gotten an opportunity like this if I moved to New York like I planned.

The drive was rather peaceful. There weren't that many

cars on the road since it was the weekend, and it was late afternoon, so most of the people my age hadn't begun their weekend debauchery. I didn't have any bad intentions on my agenda for the weekend, and I rarely mixed it up with the people my age who thought they ran the town on Friday and Saturday night. I didn't have Carson Cove *privilege* as some people referred to it—that basically meant you were filthy rich and not afraid to flaunt it.

There would be plenty of people at the auction with Carson Cove privilege, and my only goal for the evening was blending in so that I didn't look like an unprivileged member of the middle class. I wasn't ashamed of being unprivileged, but it would be nice to have one evening where I didn't get slapped in the face by it.

Tonight, I'm not simple little Taylor Abernathy from Mandalay—I'm just a girl in a black dress who enjoys art—standing next to people who could buy every piece with a wave of their hand.

One hour later

*T*he art show was set up in sections where you could browse based on the price range, and there was an area with an open bar and some snacks I would have never purchased on my own, for those who were just there to socialize. Like most gatherings in Carson Cove, it was more important for people to *know* they were getting something expensive than to just enjoy it, so there was a card explaining why everything you could have was special. The liquor they were serving was a step above top shelf, the wine was older than anyone in the room, and the snacks were ridiculously expensive.

I learned that it was possible to spend five-hundred dollars for a pound of cheese and while it wasn't bad, it didn't taste *that* good. Even the crackers were from a premium bakery that boasted about using water you could only get a certain time of day from a special spring that was supposedly prehistoric with rich deposits of Tanzanite at the bottom. The crackers didn't taste any different than the generic ones my mom bought at the grocery store, but the people around me acted like they were sampling manna from heaven.

I guess I'll get a glass of wine—it's not like I'll ever get to drink anything this expensive again.

The only good thing about the exotic food and drink selection was that nobody seemed to notice an *unprivileged* in their ranks. I was completely ignored for the most part. I started walking through the gallery and immediately wished it was socially acceptable to take pictures because some of the paintings that were being auctioned were exquisite.

I might not have had the means to hang one of them in my home, but I *loved* art. I got that from my parents—they were both artists when they were younger, and several of our family vacations were conveniently scheduled around art shows at the destination they chose. That part of our family dynamic never rubbed off on my sister, and she normally complained when our vacation took a detour towards a museum, but I couldn't have been happier.

My parents would love to be here right now—they might even be civil to each other while they were looking at all of these pieces of art.

I spent some time looking through the gallery while I sipped my wine, and by the time I got to the end of the first section, I decided that I wanted a refill. I hated to admit that it was the best wine I had ever tasted, although my palate was inexperienced. There were more people near the open bar than there were when I got my first glass of wine, so I had to wait my turn to get served. I tried to pretend that I was a statue that only got to take a step when the person in front of me did. I was nothing more than an image against the backdrop—a nameless face in the crowd. I hoped to stay that way for the rest of the night.

The glamorous, beautiful, and drop-dead gorgeous Carson Cove privileged were all around me, and I was extremely uncomfortable. As soon as my glass was refilled, I scooted over to the side to look for an opening, so I could disappear into the gallery. I must have blended in so well that the privileged thought I was *literally* part of the scenery because two women walked over and stood directly in front of me to sip their wine while they gossiped about the other guests. I wasn't sure if they cared that someone was behind them or were just so caught up in their own conversation that they didn't notice—I couldn't help but eavesdrop.

"Did you hear that Jon and Mary Alcott are getting a divorce?" The woman on the left, a blonde in a Versace dress, leaned close to the brunette beside her. "They're here together, but this may be the last event in Carson Cove that they attend as a couple."

"Then I guess they won't be buying anything." The brunette hid her laugh behind her wine glass. "Unless they plan to take a pair of scissors to it when they split everything."

"She'll probably get custody of the kids and take him to the cleaners." The blonde shrugged. "He won't have much of anything after she's done with him.

"I'll mark him off my list of future ex-husbands." The brunette grinned and sipped her wine.

"Speaking of—do you have any leads?" The blonde gave her friend a side-eyed glance. "I never thought I'd see the day Alexis Devereaux was celebrating the anniversary of her last divorce without an engagement ring on her finger."

Oh my god! That's Alexis Devereaux? I need to get the hell away from here—asap! She is not someone I want to be associated with by accident.

"I've got my eye on someone." Alexis winked at the blonde. "I might even have our first date lined up before the end of the show—which means the countdown to taking him for half of everything he owns can officially begin."

"Cheers to that." The blonde tapped her wine glass against the one that Alexis was holding.

Alexis Devereaux was a Carson Cove legend. There were a lot of rumors about her, and most of them probably weren't true, but one of them appeared to be—if she was single, she was on the prowl. She had two ex-husbands before she was thirty and had recently divorced the third—people said it was messy. I had no idea how men kept falling into her trap—okay, scratch that—I knew *exactly* why men kept falling into her trap. She was privileged and gorgeous. That was the perfect combination in Carson Cove, but it helped if you had a side of wicked, and Alexis Devereaux definitely had that.

Oh, thank god. They're going to get more wine.

I watched as Alexis Devereaux and her blonde friend walked towards the bar—then darted into the gallery. I had already looked at the first section, so I started walking through the second one. I went slow and savored all of the artwork I would never see again. Once the auction was complete, it would be in the home of a privileged family from Carson Cove, and it was rare for them to part with anything—except spouses. I drained my glass of wine fairly quick once I started walking around, but I decided that two was more than enough. I still had to drive home after the show was over. I finished with the second section, moved on to the third, and when I was done with that, it was time to see some of the most expensive pieces that would be auctioned off.

Monet. Rembrandt. Picasso. Van Gogh. Oh my god—is that a real Michelangelo!?

I was literally walking through history. It was breathtaking. I wanted to run up to each masterpiece and stare at it until I memorized every brushstroke—but that would have drawn attention to the fact that I didn't belong there—so I pretended that I wasn't impressed. It was one of the most difficult things that I had ever done, but somehow—I made it. I passed the other two students from Carson Cove University that had won tickets, and they weren't being very subtle, which got them a few disapproving stares from the privileged. I had successfully managed to blend in, and there was enough time to take another tour if I wanted, so I decided that another glass of wine wouldn't hurt if I was going to be staying for a while.

Oh wow—that's Mr. Benson. I wonder if I should say hello…

Mr. Benson preferred to be called Bryant—he had told me that at least a dozen times. He was one of the privileged, but he was very down to earth. I knew that because his youngest daughter, Victoria, has been my best friend since elementary school. I never felt like I was *just* middle class when I hung out at the Benson Estate—they treated me like a member of the family. They even let me go on vacation with them one year when their oldest daughter decided to spend the summer with her grandparents. That seemed like a lifetime ago—when there was a Mrs. Benson—before she decided to leave her husband.

I still don't know how she could leave someone as amazing as him…

I had a bit of a crush on Bryant when I was younger. He was incredibly attractive—and the touch of gray in his beard had made him even *hotter*—if that was possible. Just looking at him made my temperature rise and my throat dry out, so I decided to get another glass of wine before I said hello. There was a line, just like the last time, so I waited my turn. It took several minutes to get to the bar, and when I turned back towards Bryant, he wasn't alone. Alexis Devereaux was standing next to him—no, she was *flirting* with him. Her hand was on his wrist—she was giggling like a schoolgirl—and I finally understood what it meant when someone said that a woman had *fuck me* eyes.

Alex Devereaux's target—is Victoria's father? Oh my god…

Chapter Two

BRYANT

Earlier that day

"*M*r. Benson? Don't forget that you have the art show tonight." My secretary, Cassie, knocked on my office door and pushed it open.

"The art show. Right." I nodded and leaned back in my chair as a sigh rushed across my lips.

Fuck. That's the last place I want to go today.

"You can buy me a Rembrandt to hang above my desk if you want." She raised her eyebrows and grinned.

"No." I narrowed my eyes and growled, which caused her to make a swift exit.

It was bad enough that an emergency at Benson Enterprises forced me to bring some of my staff in on a Saturday, but I wasn't even going to be able to relax when I finally sent them home. I had to put in an appearance at Wellington's to pretend like I needed to see the stuff I planned to buy at the annual art auction. I already knew which pieces I was going to bring home with me—hell, I requested them from Mr. Wellington personally. The auction was just a formality so that everyone felt like they were getting a fair shot at them and avoid the perception of favoritism. I wasn't his only client, and it was a good cause, so I didn't mind overpaying since some of the proceeds were going to charity.

Mr. Wellington has been good to me, so I guess I can put a smile on my face for a few hours.

Several hours later

"Okay, everyone—listen up." I walked out of my office and positioned myself so that everyone could see me. "We're going to call it a day. I think we're as caught up as we're going to get on a Saturday. I'm sorry I took you away from your family on the weekend, but I'll make sure you all get a bonus on your next check to make up for it."

"Thank you, Mr. Benson." An employee named Charles leaned forward in his chair and gave a nod.

"No, thank you." I pointed at him and turned back towards my office.

"Do I get a bonus too?" Cassie looked up from her desk and tried to give me her best impression of puppy-dog eyes.

"I already pay you too much," I growled under my breath. "Yes, you'll get a bonus too."

"Thank you." Her face lit up with a huge smile.

"Yeah, yeah…" I shook my head and walked past her desk. "Why don't you send me my schedule for next week before you go, so I can look over it."

"Did something else come up?" Her voice echoed concern.

"I might want to move some stuff around." I slammed my door and chuckled under my breath.

I should actually do it just to annoy the fuck out her…

I wasn't really planning to move anything on my schedule

—I just wanted to make sure I was prepared for Monday. Truthfully, I was just stalling for time. There was nothing wrong with being fashionably late to the art show if I could blame it on work. I couldn't even claim a family emergency with all of my kids in college and my wedding band at the bottom of Carson Bay—where I threw it after the love of my life told me that she wanted a divorce. Half the people in Carson Cove had at least one divorce to go with the skeletons in their closet, but I thought my marriage was going to last—I didn't even realize there was a problem until it was too late. I had to take my share of the blame once I heard why she was unhappy. I just wished she would have said something before she was ready to call it quits.

I can't avoid the art show forever—I might as well head that way before fashionably late becomes disrespectfully absent.

Every social event in Carson Cove was an excuse for people with too much money to dress up, show off their latest arm candy, and vulgarize their wealth. I hated it. I tried to raise my kids to appreciate the friendships they made, regardless of social class, and do what they were passionate about instead of what was supposedly expected.

My youngest daughter, Victoria, seemed to get it, but she was the only one. My other two kids fell victim to temptation—and Carson Cove was full of them. It wasn't like I could say anything. My wisdom came with experience. When I was their age, I didn't know any better either—even though my father gave me the same speech I gave them and had to watch it bounce off my thick head.

Time to pretend I give a fuck about all of this.

My first stop when I walked into Wellington's museum was the bar. If there was one benefit to attending the art show, it was the Scotch. Mr. Wellington knew what I liked and always made sure there was a bottle behind the bar with my name on it. I grabbed my first drink and said hello to a few people so that my presence would be noticed. After that, I started browsing the high-end pieces that were going to be auctioned.

I feigned indifference for the pieces that I planned to buy, and paid careful attention to the ones that I didn't have any interest in—it was nothing more than a game—if I showed interest, others would wonder if they were missing out on something and that helped Mr. Wellington.

"You're thinking about the Rembrandt?" Jon Alcott—one of my closest friends and a client I managed money for—walked up beside me.

"Yeah, it's interesting." I nodded. "I believe it is from his later years…"

I hate this painting. I prefer the stuff he did in his prime. Jon knows my tricks—he would be doing the same thing under different circumstances.

"I wish I could bid on it—but, I'm sure you've heard…" He sighed and shook his head.

"Yeah." I patted him on the back. "Sorry to hear it—we should get together and talk about it sometime. I've been through that myself…"

I always liked Mary—she was a lot of fun when she was sixteen— too bad she grew up to be an ice-cold bitch.

"Thanks." Jon looked down at his glass. "I need a refill. How about you?"

"Yeah." I drained what was left of my Scotch. "Let's take care of that."

Jon and I grew up together. We attended Carson Cove Academy—played on the football team—hell, we even won the State Championship the year we graduated. We were practically brothers once upon a time, but those days were long behind us. Our gridiron success didn't carry over to college— mainly because we decided to stay local and go to Carson Cove University instead of accepting one of the scholarships we had to a *football* university.

Our futures were already set for us, so the field didn't really matter after high school. I was destined to sit in my father's chair at Benson Enterprises. Jon was destined to do the same at Alcott Inc. It was too bad neither of those paths led to the happily ever after we thought we were going to get.

"Alexis Devereaux is on the prowl." Jon motioned to the brunette that was working the crowd like she was the only human being on the planet that mattered.

"Oh?" I raised an eyebrow.

"You know she won't be single for long—maybe you should go for it." Jon nudged me and chuckled.

"Yeah, I don't know about that…" I sipped my Scotch and stared.

Alexis Devereaux was every man's wet dream when we were in high school. She was two years older than us, the hottest thing in heels, and she knew how to make a man beg—hell, she *loved* making them beg. I took a shot once when I felt Cupid's poisoned arrow and got turned down on the spot. She married young—divorced young—got married again—and history repeated itself.

Her next marriage would be her fourth, and I was pretty sure she had no intention of making it her last. She didn't even bother to change her last name when she got married—maybe that should have been a sign. She was the last person in Carson Cove that I needed to get tangled up with. I had no intention of getting my heart broken again and fuck if that woman didn't know how to make them shatter on command.

"My soon-to-be ex-wife wants something. I guess I still have to acknowledge her." Jon finished the drink in his hand and got a refill before he walked over to Mary.

It's too early to leave. I'll take another trip through the gallery.

"Bryant!" A woman's voice echoed behind me, and I didn't have to turn around to know who it belonged to.

I should have just left—even if it is early.

"Hey Alexis." I turned around to see her walking towards me with a purpose.

"How have you been? We haven't had a chance to talk much since your divorce…" She put her hand on my wrist and slowly moved it along my forearm.

"We haven't talked at *all* since my divorce." I narrowed my eyes. "Hell, I don't think we've said more than a few words to each other since high school."

I certainly haven't tried to strike up a conversation.

"Oh, don't be silly." She threw her head back and laughed. "You were married—I'm no homewrecker."

"Is there something you want?" I tilted my head to the side. "I was just about to head to the gallery…"

"The gallery is boring." She patted my arm and took a step closer. "You already know what you're going to buy—just like I do."

"Yes…" I sighed. "Does that mean you're going to bid against me?"

"No way. I don't like to lose." She giggled—Alexis Devereaux giggled—I didn't even know that was possible.

Out of the corner of my eye, I saw someone walk up to the bar—a woman I didn't recognize. She had long honey-amber curls and a black dress that appeared to be a knock-off of a famous designer, but I couldn't remember their name—my ex-wife would have known—and swiped one of my credit cards to buy the real thing. Alexis was still babbling in my ear, but I wasn't paying attention to her— I was mesmerized. The woman at the bar had gorgeous curves, and it was almost impossible to pretend that I was listening to Alexis while trying to drink in the sight I wanted to stare at all night.

When the woman finally turned around with a glass of wine in her hand, I saw pale emerald eyes that snapped me back to reality. I did know her—I had known her since she was a little girl—there was no mistaking those haunting eyes. She was my daughter's best friend, Taylor! I haven't seen her since they graduated from high school. Realizing who she was made me immediately cut my eyes back to Alexis and pretend to give a damn about what she was saying.

Damn. Taylor is all grown up now—and she's fucking beautiful...

Chapter Three

TAYLOR

*T*he sight of Alexis Devereaux trying to work her magic on my best friend's father horrified me. It was almost impossible to grow up in Carson Cove without hearing stories about Alexis Devereaux—she had quite a reputation—she might as well have been a celebrity. Victoria definitely wasn't a fan. She dated Blake Devereaux one summer and told me that every interaction with his mother was awful—even the daughter of someone as privileged as Bryant Benson wasn't good enough for one of the Devereaux boys. Alexis seemed to have changed her stance on the Benson family if she was planning to literally marry her way into it—or maybe she just thought Bryant was an easy target with his wife out of the picture.

He's the one she was talking about... I know he's not falling for her vicious charm—he's way too smart for that. Surely, he at least suspects she is only after him for his money.

Bryant didn't look comfortable—but he wasn't telling her to pound sand like I would have done if our roles were reversed—or she just couldn't take a hint. His body language didn't seem to indicate that he was interested, but she wasn't backing down. She moved closer to him—tried to whisper something in his ear—and I saw him look around the room like he was trying to figure out how fast he could make it to the exit. There were too many people around for a quiet exit. He drained the liquor out of his glass—Scotch if I remembered what he liked correctly—and stared at the empty glass for a moment. That gave me an idea—a really *bad* idea—but I felt like I owed it to Victoria. She would never forgive me if she found out that I just stood there while her father got seduced by Alexis Devereaux.

"Ah, yes." I walked back to the bar, which thankfully didn't have a line. "Mr. Benson asked me to get him another drink—Scotch, I believe?"

"Of course." The bartender immediately reached down and picked up a bottle that was hidden under the bar. "Please remind Mr. Benson that he can pick up this bottle before he leaves."

Damn—I thought the stuff that was one step above top shelf was impressive—he's got his own bottle reserved?

"Thank you." I picked up the glass of Scotch and turned around.

It felt like someone else was guiding each step as I closed the distance between the bar and the horrific sight of Alexis Devereaux trying to work her magic on Victoria's father. If the rumors were true, once she set her sights on a man, they were already hers—even if they didn't know it yet. I wanted to believe Bryant would never fall for a woman with venom dripping from her breath, but I was afraid of what would happen if he did. Victoria told me that her father had been rather vulnerable since her mother divorced him—and quite lonely. That sounded like a horrible combination that a woman like Alexis Devereaux could take advantage of—but maybe I could give him the space he needed before she buried her fangs in his neck.

I owe Victoria that much at least...

Bryant saw me coming before I got there—our eyes met, and I couldn't tell if he was relieved or confused. Alexis wasn't paying attention to anyone in the room except him—a train could have probably barreled through the gallery with horns blaring, and she wouldn't have stopped trying to seduce him.

"There you are." I walked up beside him. "I thought you forgot all about me—I got you another drink."

"Thank you." His eyes were still resonating with confusion —or maybe it had shifted to intrigue—I couldn't tell.

"I'm sorry, who are you?" Alexis Devereaux's head snapped back like someone had just slapped the silicone out of her cheeks.

"Hi!" I made my face light up with a smile. "I'm his date. I don't believe we've met—my name is Taylor. And you are..."

"Me?" Her eyes got wide—I knew that pretending not to know who she was would insult her—which was what I was going for. "I'm Alexis Devereaux!"

"Nice to meet you." I locked arms with Bryant and extended my hand as if her name meant nothing to me.

"I just remembered that I have a prior engagement." She didn't shake my hand. "Bryant, it was wonderful to catch up with you—another time, perhaps?"

"Of course." Bryant gave her a polite nod and then she immediately walked towards the door—I couldn't help but notice that her blonde friend went scurrying in that direction as well.

"I'm sorry." I looked up at him. "You looked like you could use a friend."

"More than ever..." He exhaled sharply and sipped his Scotch.

"The bartender said I should remind you to pick up your bottle before you go." I smiled and sipped my wine.

"I think I might need it tonight." He shook his head and

chuckled under his breath. "How have you been? What are you doing here?"

"I've been good." I nodded quickly. "I won a raffle at the university to attend the show—I'm in the art program there."

"That's right." He nodded. "I remember Victoria mentioning that you were staying in Carson Cove for college—but art? Why art?"

"You don't remember that time Victoria and I turned her bedroom wall into a mural?" I looked down and smiled.

That didn't end well.

"I do." He chuckled and took a sip of his Scotch. "Hopefully you've gotten better at drawing stick figures since then…"

"I'd like to believe that I have." I sipped my wine and laughed. "Sadly, I'll probably just end up doing graphic design instead of painting masterpieces."

"You never know." He raised an eyebrow. "I might be bidding on a Taylor Abernathy instead of a Pablo Picasso one day."

"You would probably be the only one bidding…" I shook my head back and forth, but I couldn't hide my smile—I might have even blushed.

"I'd love to see your work sometime—seriously." He furrowed his brow and nodded.

"Maybe…" I shrugged. "I haven't really shown it to anyone."

He's probably just being nice…

"Then I'll be your first critic." He lifted his glass and took a sip.

"It looks like the coast is clear." I let my hand fall away from Bryant's arm. "It's probably time for me to go."

"Go?" Bryant raised his eyebrows. "You just got a glass of wine—surely you weren't planning on leaving."

I forgot how perceptive he is—Victoria and I were never able to get away with anything when he was around.

"I was *considering* another trip through the gallery." I didn't have much choice but to admit the truth. "I don't get to see paintings like this very often."

"I wouldn't be a very good *date* if I let you leave before you were finished looking at everything." He extended the crook of his arm. "Let's go."

"Okay..." I nodded and put my hand back where it was when I pretended to claim him in front of the Carson Cove sycophant.

He led me into the gallery—and I was no longer invisible. I was on Bryant Benson's arm—that caused a few murmurs as we walked past the people who had previously ignored me. I started to wonder if I had made a mistake. I didn't want to be noticed. I questioned if there was any way that Bryant would have actually fallen for Alexis Devereaux's vicious charm—but he seemed to be relieved when I ran her off. I fulfilled whatever obligation I had to Victoria once she walked away, but I was still there—admiring paintings in the gallery with a man who could have bought every single one of them if he wanted—a man that I used to have a crush on when I was younger. The years had certainly been kind of him—he was still the most attractive man I had ever laid eyes on.

"Pretend that you're admiring the Rembrandt." Bryant came to a stop and stared at the painting in front of us.

"It's—amazing." I didn't have to pretend.

I doubt I'll be this close to one again.

"Yes, but while everyone is taking notes about the Rembrandt, I'm looking at the Picasso." He gave me a slight wink.

"I've never been a big fan of Picasso..." I cut my eyes towards the painting he was actually looking at.

"He found beauty in chaos—then turned beauty *into* chaos." Bryant closed his eyes for a moment. "He saw the world through eyes that nobody will ever truly understand."

"That does describe his work pretty well…" I nodded.

"The painting Mr. Wellington is auctioning this year is from the Rose Period. I prefer the stuff he did in his later years, but I'll never turn down the opportunity to hang a Picasso in my house." Bryant lifted his shoulders with a slight shrug.

"Everyone has their tastes." I looked up at him and smiled. *That came out wrong…*

"Indeed…" His eyes met mine, and they lingered there for a moment—then he looked towards the next painting. "Let's move on before someone figures out that I'm just trying to lure them into bidding on the Rembrandt."

I started to get nervous as we continued to walk through the gallery. It felt like there were *way* too many eyes on me. Bryant didn't seem to notice, but I certainly did. I was just trying to do my best friend's father a favor—I didn't want to become a topic of conversation. I told him what I overheard Alexis saying while we walked—and he didn't seem to be *that* surprised by her ulterior motives. Maybe he saw through her from the beginning—he knew a *lot* more about her than I did.

I was glad to be out of the gallery once we made it back to the bar area. Most of the people were socializing and didn't seem to notice that Bryant had someone on his arm. My glass was empty, and I definitely wasn't going to have more wine. I just needed to find a way to make a graceful exit. My night had taken a turn that I didn't see coming when I walked into the art show, but it was time for it to end. I didn't belong amongst the privileged.

"I really should be going now." I put my empty glass down on the table beside me.

"I've put in an appearance, so I'm ready to call it a night too." He looked towards the bar. "Let me grab my bottle of Scotch, and I'll walk you to your car."

"Okay." I nodded and stayed on his arm as we walked up to the bar.

A few of the people that had previously ignored us in the bar area took notice when we started walking towards the door —and I heard a few whispers. It would have probably been better if I had left on my own, but I was supposed to be his date for the evening—as far as Alexis Devereaux was concerned. A few rumors might be enough to keep her far away from Bryant. It wasn't like anyone there knew who I really was—I didn't have a name that carried any weight in Carson Cove. I went to school with some of their kids, but most of them ignored me too. I wouldn't have been able to match the family trees together if they were standing in front of me—and I preferred it that way.

"That's my car." I pointed at the Toyota Corolla, which stood out like a sore thumb amongst the luxurious cars that surrounded it.

"Should I pick you up, or will you meet me there?" Bryant turned towards me once I got to my car.

"I'm sorry—what?" I nearly dropped my keys as I pulled them out of my purse and hit the button to unlock my door.

"The auction." He tilted his head with an expression on his face that indicated I should have known what he meant without needing an explanation.

"I'm not going to the auction." I quickly shook my head back and forth. "I won a raffle ticket to come to the art show— the auction is for people who actually intend to bid on those masterpieces."

"People who plan to bid..." He nodded. "...and their dates."

"I wasn't *really* your date." I looked down and felt my face get warm—I was definitely blushing.

"You are now," he chuckled under his breath. "Alexis will be at the auction, and I could use the back-up."

"I think you can handle her on your own." I looked up at

him, and a half-smile formed on the edge of my lips. "You already know that she's just after you for your money."

I would prefer not to be on her radar—I've heard that everyone who crosses her regrets it. Maybe I should have thought about that before I introduced myself...

"Why risk it?" He shrugged. "Especially when I could have someone as beautiful as you on my arm the entire night."

Beautiful? Me? Surely, he's just being nice...

"You really want me to go?" I raised my eyebrows and studied his expression.

"Absolutely." His response came without a hint of hesitation. "I promise you'll have fun."

"Okay..." I nodded. "I definitely don't have anything going on that night."

Or any other night—unless I have an assignment for school that I need to work on.

"Then it's settled. I'll pick you up at six." He leaned forward and opened my door—he was so close to me that I could feel the heat resonating from his body.

"Six..." I repeated what he said for no reason at all—and then quickly sat down in my car.

I just agreed to be his date for the auction. I should have declined—I could have done it politely.

Bryant waited until I was seated and then pushed the door closed. He gave me a slight nod—and then started walking towards his car. I tried to process what had just transpired as I cranked up my car and put it in drive. I never expected a man like him to call me *beautiful*—that was for damn sure. I reminded myself more than once that he was Victoria's father as I drove towards my subdivision—there was no way anything could ever happen between us. I had a crush on him when I was younger, but it was harmless—I never expected him to see me as anything more than a teenage girl that was friends with his daughter. I wasn't a teenager anymore, but Victoria was still my best friend. It didn't matter if my heart raced when Bryant looked at me—or my stomach twisted into a knot when he called me beautiful—he was *totally* off-limits. Nothing could change that.

I'll be his date for the auction, but that's it. Once it's over, I'll go back to being the normal girl I've always been—the girl that doesn't exist in the world of the privileged.

Chapter Four

BRYANT

Two hours later

$\mathcal{I}$ needed to be in bed—not sitting in my living room, enjoying another glass of Scotch while I tried to sort through the events of the evening in my head. The people that worked for me had Sunday off, but I didn't really get a day to completely shut myself off from Benson Enterprises. There was always something that needed my attention. I might have cut myself a break if I was sitting on my couch thinking about work, but that wasn't the case. I was thinking about Alexis Devereaux—and the beautiful Taylor that made Alexis seethe.

It was quite satisfying to see Alexis get knocked off her pedestal and storm out of the art show. She wasn't the kind of woman that just accepted defeat though, and I knew she was already planning her revenge. Taylor wasn't from one of the so-called privileged families in Carson Cove, so there wasn't much that Alexis could do to her if she felt like she had been insulted.

Even if she could—I wouldn't let her.

There was something about Taylor that drew me in like I

was a moth circling a flame—and I was going to get burned if I let my thoughts get out of control. Taylor was all grown up. She wasn't a kid anymore. She was always pretty, but I never saw her as anything more than my daughter's best friend. I certainly wasn't attracted to her back then—but the years had been kind to her, while they were cruel to me. The last time I saw Taylor, she was walking across the stage to get her high school diploma—while the woman I loved was clapping alongside me. I had no idea that it would be the last event we attended together as husband and wife. I certainly didn't realize that I was weeks away from hurling my wedding band into Carson Bay.

Now the memories are just fucking with me. I'm going to bed.

Two days later

"*D*id you buy anything at the art show?" Cassie met me at the elevator with a cup of coffee in her hand.

"The auction is tomorrow." I took the cup of coffee from her. "The art show was just an excuse to get all of the bidders together ahead of time, so we could see everything beforehand."

"I figured you would still find a way to take a few pieces home." She shrugged. "Like the Rembrandt you're going to hang on the wall behind my desk…"

"That's not going to happen, Cassie," I growled under my breath. "Let it go."

"Fine…" She rolled her eyes and sighed. "You've got a meeting at nine—the notes are on your desk."

"Thank you." I nodded and walked towards my office.

Cassie was a secretary with dreams of doing more than fetching my coffee and organizing my calendar. She just didn't have the drive to make it happen—she expected things to be handed to her. If she could have conquered the world by pouting, she would have been crowned queen a long time ago.

Unfortunately, people like her were a dime a dozen in Carson Cove. She was good at her job, so I put up with her antics most of the time—but she knew where the line was, which set her apart from most of the others that had sat behind that desk. I knew she was mostly joking about the Rembrandt, but there was a tiny sliver of hope that I would just cave and give her what she wanted—that's what her father always did. Her family never had much, but they spoiled her, and she expected everyone else to do the same damn thing.

She's the perfect example of what happens when you give people something for nothing—that's why I raised my kids to work for what they got even though they didn't have to.

My day was spent tending to things at Benson Enterprises —just like every other day. There was nothing glamorous about running an investment firm in Carson Cove. I grew up idolizing my father because he seemed to be the most popular man in town—everyone loved him, and they treated him with respect. Then I got to see the ugly side of the people that pretended he was their best friend when a recession hit—it was an economic downturn that he couldn't control, but they certainly acted like their losses were all his fault. The stress took a toll on my father, and I had to bury him long before his time because of it. I thought the day I took over as CEO of Benson Enterprises would be a joyous one—instead, it just left me with a bitter taste in my mouth for all of the clients that became my responsibility.

It was only a matter of time before that bitterness spilled over into my personal life—I just didn't realize it would destroy my marriage until it was too late.

The next day

*M*r. Wellington called me before the auction to make sure I got his email with the itinerary for the evening. Everyone in Carson Cove that had enough money to make a serious bid got one of those calls. Mr. Wellington was pushing seventy and had an old school mentality when it came to customer service. That was part of the reason he entertained my requests when it was time for another auction. I could have approached the people who wanted to sell the paintings personally, but I preferred to let Mr. Wellington auction them off. It ensured that some of the profits went to charity and kept the museum in business. I believed in giving back to the community—even if there were a few residents that I wasn't entirely fond of due to how they treated my father.

"Why are you still here?" I adjusted my tie as I walked out of my office and was surprised to see Cassie sitting at her desk.

"I was just working on a few things for tomorrow—I'm leaving early, remember?" She looked up at me.

"Ah, that's right." I nodded as I remembered her asking to leave early for an appointment—hair or nails if memory served.

"Good luck at the auction. I hope you get some good pieces." She turned back towards her computer.

She must actually be trying to get some work done if she isn't going to make one final plea for a Rembrandt to hang over her desk—or maybe she realizes that the joke has run its course.

My office wasn't that far from the Mandalay Subdivision where Taylor lived. I had dropped her off after a weekend at my place enough to remember which house belonged to her family. I started to get a worried feeling in my stomach when I made the right turn on Cherry Street—if I was picking her up for a date, it was usually customary to knock on the front door. I had no idea how Mrs. Abernathy would feel about me showing up at her house —with every intention of taking her daughter on a date. Taylor wasn't a kid anymore, but she was still her mother's little girl. Her gorgeous curves didn't change that—as tempting as they were.

It looks like I might get to avoid that meeting after all—Taylor is waiting on me in her driveway. Damn, she looks even better than she did the other night.

"I hope you haven't been waiting long." I looked at my watch as I stepped out of my car—I was one minute early.

"No, I just figured it would be easier to wait for you out here—for obvious reasons." She smiled and started walking towards my car.

"That thought did cross my mind." I walked around my car and opened the passenger side door. "I don't think your mother would approve of this—date…"

"She hasn't made it home from work yet." Taylor leaned forward and sat down in the passenger seat. "You're in the clear."

We both seemed to have a fundamental understanding of the fact that the date was inherently *wrong*, but that didn't erase the mutual attraction. Maybe I was more attracted to her than she was to me, but there were looks—lingering stares—I noticed them out of the corner of my eye. I kept my eyes on the road for the majority of the drive, but I couldn't help letting them wander a couple of times—her dress was shorter than the one she wore to the art show—and the neckline showed off a hint of cleavage.

"What's the game plan when we get to the auction? Should I just stay on your arm all night and flash Alexis Devereaux a dirty look if she tries to talk to you?" Taylor looked over at me and smiled.

"That should work," I chuckled under my breath. "I think she'll realize she doesn't stand a chance when she sees you in that dress. You're going to make a lot of women think about calling their plastic surgeon before the night is over."

"Should I have worn something different?" She looked down with a hint of worry in her pale green eyes.

"No." I shook my head back and forth. "You look beautiful —hell, you're fucking gorgeous."

And you're even more beautiful when a compliment makes you blush.

I managed to draw a line in my head between the girl that I used to know, and the woman Taylor had become. They might have been one in the same, but I let my attraction blind me to everything except for the woman sitting next to me. I hadn't been on a date with anyone since my divorce, but Taylor made me feel things that I thought I would never feel again. The world seemed to be a little more vibrant—the air tasted cleaner —and the bleakness in my soul didn't crush my spirit like it normally did. Alexis Devereaux couldn't compete with that— nobody could.

Unfortunately, the reality of the situation was too strong to just ignore the fact that she was my daughter's best friend. She was my date for the auction, but that was all she could ever be. Once the night was over, I would have to accept that—one date with Taylor was all that I would ever be able to have—and it was a fabricated one, designed to keep Alexis Devereaux at bay. Her charm might have captivated me in high school, but I wasn't stupid enough to believe that she was after anything more than another rich husband she could plunder in an expensive divorce. She would have annoyed me for a little longer at the art show if Taylor hadn't walked over, but she wouldn't have gotten what she wanted.

"Valet parking?" Taylor raised her eyebrow as we pulled up to the curb outside of the museum. "They didn't have that for the art show."

"Mr. Wellington likes to turn it into a grand affair," I chuckled under my breath.

We were early—technically. The itinerary said the auction was supposed to start at seven o'clock, but the first piece wouldn't be brought out any earlier than eight. That gave people time to have a drink or two—and lower their inhibitions when it was time to bid. I didn't need to have mine lowered—I already knew what I was going to buy.

Taylor and I got drinks from the bar and waited for the auction to begin. I was kind of relieved when I didn't see Alexis anywhere in the room. She was a great excuse to get Taylor on my arm for the evening, but it would be even better if she didn't show up at the auction. She was a fierce bidder, and her careless attempts at beating me for a piece of art had forced me to pay more than I expected a few times over the years—although I wasn't sure how she was doing financially since her last divorce. She was one of the few people in Carson Cove that didn't use my firm to manage her investments—it was probably because she blew her money so fast, she didn't have any to invest—she never was the type to plan for the future.

"I see Alexis Devereaux's blonde friend." Taylor squeezed my arm and motioned to a woman that was mingling with a couple of people in the crowd.

"Ah, yes." I nodded. "That's Gina Harrington. They were best friends in high school."

"Harrington?" Taylor raised an eyebrow. "I remember a couple of Harrington's from high school."

"Probably her brood," I chuckled under my breath. "She got married right after high school and has somehow managed to avoid the divorce-curse in Carson Cove."

"I think they're about to bring out the first piece of art for the auction." Taylor motioned to the stage.

"Yes, it looks that way. Ready to sit down?" I pulled out my phone to check which two seats had been assigned to me.

"Sure." Taylor smiled—but then the smile faded from her face as quickly as it appeared. "She's here…"

I followed Taylor's gaze and saw Alexis Devereaux walk into the room. There was a time when every eye in the room would have been on her the instant she made an appearance, but she didn't seem to get that kind of reaction anymore. Gina noticed her arrival and went scurrying to her side, just like she used to do when they were in high school together. It only took me a couple of seconds to realize that Gina had been sent to the auction early to spy on us—because she whispered something to Alexis and then they both looked our way. I decided that the best course of action was to just ignore them and tried to pull Taylor towards our seats, but she didn't budge.

"Don't give them any attention. That's what they're looking for." I gave Taylor's arm a gentle tug.

"I thought she would back off after the art show…" Taylor finally turned towards me and sighed.

"That's not her style, but I can handle Alexis. Let's just enjoy the auction." I shrugged.

"Maybe she needs a little more motivation to stay away from you…" Taylor lifted her head and grinned.

"She'll set her sights on someone else once she realizes that I'm not interested. She wants an easy target—I'm not it." I shrugged again.

"Let's see if we can speed that process along…" Taylor bit down on her bottom lip—and then she reached up to grab the back of my head.

I didn't realize that Taylor was going to kiss me until her lips were already moving towards mine. I could have pulled away—but deep down—I didn't want to. I had been thinking about those soft, pouty lips since the moment I laid eyes on them. They crashed into mine, and I didn't hesitate to kiss her back. I pulled her close—turned that sweet little kiss into one that crushed her lips and didn't stop until our tongues were intertwined. Her nails dug into my arm—she melted into my embrace—and by the time our lips broke the seal that had formed, we were both gasping for air. I didn't look to see if Alexis noticed—I didn't give a fuck. I just wanted to taste those lips again—no matter how *wrong* it was.

That look in Taylor's eyes says she wants the exact same thing—and more.

Chapter Five

"*W*e should probably go to our seats now…" I felt like I was rooted in place, and my head was still spinning from the kiss.

"Yeah…" Bryant exhaled sharply and nodded.

We stared at each other for a couple of seconds before we finally walked to our seats. My thoughts were jumbled, and I couldn't even focus on the first piece of art when it was auctioned off. I used Alexis Devereaux's arrival as an excuse to do what I had wanted to do since Bryant walked me to my car after the art show. I convinced myself that I could be his date for the auction and that would be the end of it—but I let my imagination get away from me. I wasn't a little girl crushing on my best friend's hot-dad anymore—it had turned into more than that—especially when I saw how he looked at me. Just being close to him made my pulse race, and my heart beat out of control. Kissing him made me quiver—and I was tingling from head to toe when he reached over and took my hand once we were seated.

I need to get these thoughts out of my head—it doesn't matter if I'm attracted to him. That kiss needs to be our last…

The auction appeared to be a fashion show for the Carson Cove privileged, just like the art show. I felt like the most underdressed woman in the room, but it was hard not to feel that way with so much *privilege* surrounding me—some of the dresses I saw probably cost more than my entire closet. There were a couple of waiters in tuxedos walking around to top off drinks. Even the auction paddles we got at the door were fancy —they were crafted from mahogany with the Wellington's logo burned into the front and the date of the auction on the back.

"I'm going to bid on this one." Bryant winked at me when Mr. Wellington's assistants rolled the Picasso to the middle of the stage.

"Good luck." I looked at him and smiled.

Mr. Wellington went through a brief description of the painting, and then he asked for the first bid. Bryant didn't raise his auction paddle immediately. He kept it in his lap and waited until a couple of others started to bid—then he made his intentions known. All he had to do was raise his auction paddle to scare off several of the other people who thought they were going to take the Picasso home with them. It seemed like they admitted defeat immediately—Bryant simply *commanded* the room to cower when he made his first bid. Seeing that was kind of hot—I had never seen that many wealthy people wilt before my eyes before. A couple of people bid against him, but he quickly raised it out of their price range. It looked like the Picasso was his—until I saw a paddle that hadn't been raised before lift—and the icy glare of Alexis Devereaux focused on us.

"Fuck…" Bryant muttered under his breath and raised his paddle. "She's going to drive the price up and make me spend way more than I expected…"

"What a bitch." I narrowed my eyes and met Alexis' icy glare with the best one I could muster—I don't know if I actually looked intimidating or not.

"I'll make her pay for it, don't worry." Bryant raised his paddle to continue his monetary war with Alexis.

Alexis and Bryant traded bids until she finally turned around in a huff and let him have the Picasso. It was wheeled to the side, and then they auctioned off a few pieces that weren't quite as valuable as the one he was taking home. Alexis didn't look happy that she was forced to back off—she kept cutting her eyes over at us. I responded by leaning against Bryant—playing with his hair—letting my finger drift along the side of his neck and up to his ear. It might have been just for show, but I could sense his breathing getting heavier, and I could see the hairs standing on end when my finger caressed his ear. It was enough to get another icy glare from Alexis— and then I felt Bryant's hand on my thigh—moving to the edge of my dress—teasing the inside of my thigh. Nobody could see what he was doing to me—it wasn't just for show.

I may have started something I can't finish—oh god, what was I thinking?

"There's the bait I was waiting for." Bryant pulled his hand away and leaned forward.

"The Rembrandt?" I looked at him in surprise. "I thought you didn't want that one..."

"Alexis doesn't know that." He gave me a quick wink.

Bryant had explained that the Rembrandt was just a decoy —he expected people to bid high on that painting if they truly wanted it because they knew he would be raising his paddle in response. I noticed that a few high rollers—people that had the same clout as Bryant—start bidding immediately. Bryant let them cast a few bids, then entered the fray, which immediately drew the attention of Alexis Devereaux.

For a woman who wanted to marry a rich husband and take him for half of his net worth, she seemed to already have plenty of money to burn. I wasn't an expert, but I had a pretty good idea what a Rembrandt would sell for, and they passed that figure quickly. Bryant studied Alexis while she bid against him, and when her paddle wavered, but still rose up to stop him from winning—he immediately backed off.

"Oh god…" I watched Alexis immediately go from confident to bewildered—and then she looked around the room like she was trying to find the nearest exit. "She didn't expect to win."

"No," Bryant chuckled under his breath. "She was just running the price up—and she thought I would keep going until I won."

"Now she has to actually pay for it." I leaned back, and a smile spread across my face. "That's genius."

"Yep." Bryant nodded. "Even if she wants to unload it, she'll still take a hit—it's not worth *that* much."

"I think she's officially done with this auction…" I watched as Alexis gathered her things and started walking towards the door.

"She's probably going to call her accountant and figure out just how bad she got screwed." Bryant grinned. "Serves her right."

As soon as the bidding on the next painting started, Bryant's hand returned to my thigh. There was no reason for it to be there. Alexis was gone—not that she could have seen it from where she was previously sitting anyway. I started to tingle from head to toe again when his hand moved along my inner thigh—his touch practically set me on fire. I could feel my panties getting wet—and the further he moved up my thigh, the wetter they got.

I finally had to push his hand away when my thighs were exposed, and I was afraid someone would actually notice. I didn't really *want* him to stop, but I was terrified that someone would look over their shoulder and see his hand underneath my dress. I was blushing and quite flustered when I pulled my dress down, and if he had tried again—I don't know that I would have been able to resist his touch.

"I'm going to bid on this one." Bryant leaned forward and waited for Mr. Wellington to open the bidding.

I barely paid attention when the bids started. My wine glass was empty, and my throat was dry, but I didn't think I could stand—I was afraid my knees would buckle. I had no idea what I would do when his hands found their way back to my body when we were alone. A war was being waged inside me—on one side was the understanding that *anything* between us was wrong. On the other side was a virgin with a *very* wet pair of panties that was craving his forbidden touch. Something that taboo shouldn't have felt that good—it shouldn't have been so confusing. I was no longer crushing on my best friend's father —I was lusting after the hottest guy in Carson Cove—and I knew his desires mirrored my own.

How will I ever be able to look Victoria in the eyes again if I let this go any further? It's already gone too far...

"This is the last piece." Bryant motioned to the stage. "Then we go somewhere that doesn't have an audience."

Oh god...

The auction came to a close, and people started filing out of the room. Bryant stood and offered me his hand, which I took. I caught a glimpse of Gina in the corner of my eye—she had her phone out and was furiously texting someone. I assumed Alexis was still getting a play-by-play, even though she left the auction early. It seemed pointless for her to still care— we had put on enough of a show that she should have understood she had no chance of turning Bryant into her latest victim—but deep down, I knew what happened between us wasn't just for show.

"Are we supposed to return these?" I held up my auction paddle and looked at Bryant.

"Nah, they're a souvenir." Bryant shook his head back and forth as we walked towards the exit.

I was scared to ask where he planned to take me because I didn't think I would be able to tell him *no*. The side of me that understood how inherently wrong everything that was happening between us was just didn't have the willpower to resist his charm—or his touch. I was in over my head and sinking fast. There was no way that I was going to be able to come up for air if he kissed me again—and I found out how true that realization was the instant we were in the car. He didn't just crush my lips—he devoured them.

The tint on his windows was dark enough to hide what was going on inside the car, especially in the darkness, but I don't think I would have been able to push him away—there were plenty of people in the parking lot that had already seen us kiss.

"Would you like to come back to my place?" Bryant moved his lips to my ear, and I felt the heat from his breath. "I've got plenty of wine—bottles that are much better than what they were serving at the auction."

"Bryant..." I exhaled sharply and managed to start forming thoughts that resembled something rationale. "I can't..."

"Are you sure?" He teased my ear with a gentle kiss and moved his lips down to my neck.

"I'm sorry..." I sighed and fought against the side of me that didn't want him to stop. "You should probably just take me home."

"Okay." He leaned back, and our eyes met—then he kissed my forehead. "Same time tomorrow—for our next date?"

"I doubt you're going to have worry about Alexis anymore..." I felt a lump rising up in my throat and quickly tried to swallow it.

"I don't give a damn about Alexis." He narrowed his eyes. "I just want to see you again. Can I?"

Yes? No? I don't know...

I didn't give Bryant an answer. He must have seen the conflict, and maybe he was waging a similar war because he didn't push for one. He drove through Carson Cove, and I watched the scenery zip by—mainly because I was afraid of looking over at Bryant—I was terrified of the connection we shared. A sense of dread started to get tangled up with my desire when we reached the Mandalay Subdivision, and both feelings got more intense when his car turned on Cherry Street. I didn't want the night to end—I definitely wanted to see him again—but it was too complicated for me to give in to either one of those desires.

"Wait..." I finally turned towards Bryant. "You should probably stop a couple of houses down."

"Why?" He looked over at me as he removed his foot from the gas pedal and let the car start to coast.

"My mom should be home by now. She'll ask questions if I get dropped off by someone driving a Maserati." I looked down and sighed.

"Okay." He nodded and brought the car to stop.

He didn't question that. We both understand how wrong this is...

"I had fun tonight." I lifted my head and forced a smile.

"Me too," he sighed.

"Thank you for taking me to the auction." I reached for the door.

"Hold on..." Bryant reached over and put his hand on my arm.

I turned back towards him, and I already knew he was going to kiss me before I saw him moving towards me. Bryant's lips crashed into mine—devoured them—and it made every single complication fade away for a moment. I felt his hand on my left breast. He gave it a gentle squeeze, and the nipple turned into a hard nub against his touch. His hand drifted down my dress—and I felt the fire start to sizzle inside me again.

Bryant made it to my thigh and started to slide his hand underneath the fabric. I knew I needed to stop him, but I just couldn't make myself do it. His hand went further than it had at the auction—so close to my panties that it made me squirm —then he moved his hand to my inner thigh, and before I could snap myself back to reality, I felt his finger gently caressing my pussy through my panties.

"We shouldn't do this..." My body tensed up, and I broke the seal that our lips had formed.

"Do you want me to stop?" His finger found my clit and started to slowly make circles around the tight bundle of nerves.

"No..." I shuddered and leaned against his shoulder.

I was trapped in the pleasure—it destroyed every barrier I tried to put up between us. He was the first man that had ever touched me, and it felt amazing. His finger started to move faster. A pressure built up inside me. I had felt that before— when I was alone in my room—and there were a few times when those fantasies involved Bryant. Those fantasies were nothing like the real thing— his touch was incredible. It felt like my skin was sizzling. He kept his finger moving until I began to shake, and then he pulled my panties to the side, and I felt him without the silk between us. The sensation got stronger—I moaned and dug my nails into his shoulders. The pleasure quickly overwhelmed me, and I felt the orgasm begin.

"Oh god..." My head rolled back, and the bliss surged through my veins.

Bryant kept his finger moving as the orgasm peaked—he didn't stop until it began to fade. His finger gently caressed my pussy lips, he rubbed the entrance, which was still spasming from the pleasure, and then he moved my panties back where they belonged. I didn't wait to find out if he was going to kiss me again. I immediately grabbed the back of his head and found his lips with mine. The kiss was more passionate than any of the previous one we had shared. I finally found the strength to pull away and reached for the door. It was too late to escape, but I was afraid of what I would do if I stayed.

"I'll pick you up at six." He put his hand on mine before I got the door open.

"Okay." I nodded and exited his car.

I have no idea how to tell him no—I'm in serious trouble now.

Chapter Six

BRYANT

I watched as Taylor walked to her house—with a different gait than she normally had. The orgasm was over, but the lingering effects of it were still coursing through her system. I waited until she made it through her front door before I finally drove away. I had lost all willpower to fight against what we shared. I simply didn't know how. She brought things to life inside me that I never thought I would feel again—desires that I thought had died the moment I signed my divorce papers. There was a certain aura to the situation—a lingering tease of forbidden fruit—but it was so much more than that. We had a strange connection that should have never existed. I was forty-five years old—Taylor was twenty-three. I was practically twice her age—yet she made me feel like the years that separated us simply didn't exist.

I have no idea how we're going to make this work, but I'm too far gone to figure it out right now.

The next day

"*W*e've got a problem." Cassie met me at the elevator with my morning coffee in her hand.

"What kind of problem? Why am I just hearing about this now?" I took the coffee and looked around the office.

"Because the problem just arrived—and she's sitting in your office." Cassie stepped to the side, and I saw what—or rather who—she was referring to.

Why the hell is Alexis Devereaux here?

"I'll handle it," I growled under my breath.

I had no idea why Alexis was waiting in my office—she wasn't the kind of woman that generally *waited* for anyone. She certainly didn't have an appointment. I could tell that her arrival had left the employees rather tense—even Cassie, who normally wasn't bothered by much of anything. I knew why—a year before Alexis set her sights on me, she was married to Sawyer King. He accumulated his wealth at the expense of others and had put a few companies out of business with one of his hostile takeovers.

Some of the people that worked for me had been taken to the brink of bankruptcy because of him. They lost pensions they had worked their entire lives for and had 401k accounts that were heavily invested in company stock become worthless overnight. Alexis wasn't his wife anymore, but she was front and center when they watched their world crash before their eyes.

This probably feels like a bad dream to them…

"Good morning, Bryant!" Alexis looked at me with a smile on her face when I walked into my office.

"Is it?" I walked past her and sat down at my desk. "Why are you here?"

"I feel like we got off on the wrong foot the other night." She uncrossed her legs—and re-crossed them—she probably thought it was *sexy*. "We were having such a good conversation before we were so rudely interrupted."

"My date was not an interruption." I narrowed my eyes at Alexis.

"I get it. She's young and beautiful—but surely she's nothing more than a distraction." Alexis tilted her head slightly. "I've had my fair share of *rebound-fucks* after my divorce."

"Oh? Which divorce would that be?" I raised an eyebrow and hid my amusement when I saw her squirm.

"Pick one—I always marry the assholes." She looked down for a moment but quickly regained her composure. "That's why I'm not sitting across from one right now. We used to have something—don't you remember high school? You were so in love with me then, and I was just a foolish girl that couldn't see what was right in front of my eyes."

"Why are you pretending, Alexis? High school was a long time ago, and you didn't just suddenly have an epiphany." I leaned forward and sighed. "I already know that you're not interested in me—you want another rich husband that you can take to the cleaners when you file for divorce."

I'll let her wonder how I know that—she has no idea Taylor over-heard her conversation with Gina at the art show.

"So it's going to be like that, is it?" Alexis leaned back and nodded. "That's how you see me now?"

"I see what is right in front of my eyes," I growled under my breath. "I see a woman that has never looked more desperate—it's an ugly look for you."

"We could have been good friends, Bryant." Alexis leaned forward and started to stand, but I could see that she was struggling to hide her anger. "I won't sit here and be *insulted*."

"I didn't ask you to come." I watched as she walked towards the door—but she paused before she opened it.

"You're going to regret this, Bryant. I didn't want to make

it complicated." Alexis pulled the door open and immediately started walking towards the elevator.

"Have a good day, Mrs. Devereaux..." Cassie lifted her hand and waved as Alexis as she stormed by.

"Cassie, cancel my meeting this morning." I slammed my door and walked back to my desk.

I had a sick feeling in my stomach after Alexis' visit. When Taylor told me what she overheard, I thought I understood the extent of Alexis' motivations, but something wasn't sitting right with me. There were plenty of rich guys in Carson Cove—hell, you couldn't walk down Main Street without bumping into people that wouldn't even bother to bend over to pick up a hundred dollar bill. Alexis should have been loaded after divorcing Sawyer King—and that was assuming she had already blown through her illicit gains from the two husbands that got tangled up in her poisoned charm before him. She was born with a silver spoon shoved up her ass and had expensive tastes, but she was married long before her father squandered the Devereaux family fortune. There was no way she was *that* desperate.

Something else is going on, and I need to figure out what it is...

I ended up canceling several of my appointments during the day in order to make some calls to a few of my contacts. They just served to heighten my frustration. Nobody really knew what Alexis could be up to—by all accounts, she disappeared from the business world as soon as she divorced Sawyer King. I knew he had left Carson Cove after the divorce—and I doubted he would ever work with the woman who took a scalpel to his empire.

Devereaux Properties was still limping along with her brother at the helm, but the company wasn't making any noise —they didn't have the capital to make the kind of deals they used to. She had a vested interest in the company, but she wasn't involved in the day-to-day operations.

Maybe she's just fucking with me. It wouldn't be the first time, but I can't help but worry that there's more to this than what I see on the surface.

Later that day

*C*assie left early for her appointment, so I was the last one in the office. I didn't get as much work done as I should have because I let Alexis' visit distract me from what I should have been doing. She might have left me with some lingering concerns, but none of those were enough to take away from the excitement I had when it was time to pick Taylor up. I drove to Mandalay Subdivision and let my car roll to a stop before I got to her driveway.

I didn't want to drive up to her house after she said it could be a problem—we were fortunate when I picked her up for the auction, but I doubted her mother worked late every day. I couldn't help feeling like a bit of a bastard when I thought about the fact that she didn't want her mother to know she was going out with me. It was understandable, but I wasn't the kind of guy that normally ended up in those situations—not since high school when sneaking around was required in certain situations.

There she is—she's waving for me to pick her up. Maybe her mother's working late again after all.

Taylor was wearing a stunning blue dress—and my eyes didn't stay on the road when I rolled forward and came to a stop in front of her house. As soon as she climbed into the car, she kissed me—that erased every bit of concern I had—deep down, I was afraid I was going to arrive at her house and find that she came to her senses. That obviously wasn't the case. There was a hunger in her kiss, and I could tell it wasn't going to be the last one we shared before the evening was over. She kissed me until my head was spinning, but as soon as her lips left mine, I wanted to taste them again—so I did. Feeling that passion made my cock throb in my pants. My lips were tingling when I finally pulled away from our second kiss.

"We should probably go—I assume your mother could arrive at any minute?" I exhaled sharply.

"Yeah, or my sister." She nodded quickly. "She's out with friends, but I have no idea when she'll be home."

I drove—I don't know where I was going. The restaurant that I made reservations at was in the opposite direction. My head was a mess—excitement, lust, and angst that I hadn't felt since I was a teenager were all coursing through my veins at the same time. I had passed the point of dancing around the fire—it was burning me alive from the inside out. I got to the end of the Mandalay Subdivision and let my car roll to a stop. A left would take me to my house—a right would correct the wrong turns I had made and take us to the restaurant.

"Why are you waiting?" Taylor looked over at me. "There are no cars coming…"

"I made reservations at Moretti's," I sighed and started to turn towards the right.

"I'm not hungry." She bit down on her bottom lip, and I saw a hunger in her eyes—but it definitely wasn't for expensive Italian food.

"Me either…" I quickly cut the wheel in the opposite direction and hit the gas.

There's no fight left in me—maybe it was gone the moment I felt her lips on mine for the very first time.

Chapter Seven

I had been wracked with internal conflict all day long. I went through so many emotions that I thought I was going to lose my mind before it was time for my date with Bryant. It was easy to come up with reasons why I shouldn't have gotten into his car—but when I saw it on my street, all of those reasons just faded from my thoughts and were replaced by the intense desire I had to be with him again.

I swore I would never end up in the arms of a privileged guy from Carson Cove—I wasn't going to be another conquest for one of them—it was why I guarded my heart so closely and never let anyone in. Bryant made me forget all of that. He wasn't like the well-to-do guys I stayed away from in high school—and he made the things that felt so *wrong* feel so damn *right*. It was terrifying to think that the core of who I was could be stripped away, exposed, and upended with just one kiss.

I can't even pretend that I'm just faking it to keep Alexis Devereaux away from him. I know exactly where this car is going—and all I want to do is tell him to put the pedal to the floorboard.

I hadn't told Bryant that I was still a virgin. It wasn't going to be a secret much longer. We were headed to the Benson

Estate, and my panties were getting wetter by the second. I didn't want to just feel his lips on mine—or on my neck—I wanted to feel them on every square inch of my body. There was no way that I was going to get him out of my head unless I gave in to those desires—his finger made me come, but that just made me want more.

Somewhere in the back of my mind, I managed to convince myself that it would just be once—there was no way we could have an actual relationship—no way that I could ever face Victoria when I was secretly involved with her father. Giving in to that desire felt like a reset button—a way to get past constant strings of lapses in judgment that had been plaguing me since I walked up to him at the art show. It would be our secret—one that we always shared, but never revisited.

"There's nobody here—right?" I looked up at the massive iron gate that led to the estate I had been to so many times when I was younger.

"No." He shook his head back and forth. " Dylan only visits on the weekends, and those visits are usually brief—you already know where Victoria and Shaina are."

"Yeah…" I sighed and nodded.

Bryant's son was the only one of his kids that still visited Carson Cove regularly, mainly because the university he was attending was fairly close. I had seen Dylan in town a couple of times, but we never said more than *hey*—which was still more than he ever said to me when I was visiting his family's estate. Bryant's daughters were hundreds of miles away at different universities—they only came home for long holidays and a couple of months during the summer. Victoria planned to return to Carson Cove after graduation. Shaina was in law school—and had no intentions of moving back after she was done.

"Ready to go inside?" Bryant pulled the car into the garage and killed the engine.

"I…" Every reason why I shouldn't hit me all at once.

Bryant didn't let the hesitation linger long enough for it to fester and change my mind. He leaned over and started kissing me. That put all of my focus firmly on the desires that had been tearing at me since I got out of his car the previous night. His lips made mine smolder, and I melted into the kiss. He pulled me close, and I pushed him back—not because I wanted the kiss to end, but because I wanted to be closer to him.

There's no way I can stop now—the desires have consumed every rational thought I could ever have.

I crawled over into Bryant's seat, and he pushed his seat back as I straddled him. Our kiss got more intense, and when I sank into his lap, I could feel his cock throbbing in his pants. My panties were saturated, and my dress started to ride up when I spread my legs across his thighs. Bryant put his hands on my calves—moved them slowly up to my ass—and wrapped his fingers around my panties. My pulse was racing—my heart was beating harder than it had ever beat before.

"Maybe we don't have to go inside…" Bryant exhaled sharply and pulled my panties down far enough to start rubbing my pussy from behind.

"Wait…" I moaned, and the pleasure started to flood my system. "I don't want to lose my virginity in a car."

"You're—still a virgin?" Bryant's head snapped back, and his finger stopped moving.

"It's okay. I know what I want…" I pushed myself back against the steering wheel and traced his cock through his pants.

Bryant opened the car door and helped me out. His lips found mine as soon as he stood, and he started pushing me towards the door that led to the house. The key went into the lock, and then we were inside the house—our lips never separated—Bryant's tongue ravaged my mouth as I continued to sink further into the overwhelming lust that had taken hold of me. He pressed me against the counter in the kitchen—his hands went under my dress and pulled my panties down to my knees. I tensed up when his hand moved between my legs, and his finger started to rub my clit. I squirmed against the counter, and my panties fell further down my legs—then they were around my ankles and barely hanging on.

"How do you feel about losing your virginity in a kitchen?" He moved his lips to my neck and started rubbing my clit faster.

"It's—not preferred," I moaned and arched my back against the counter as I kicked my panties off.

"The living room?" Bryant pulled me forward and then started pushing me towards the doorway that separated his enormous kitchen from the spacious living room—he didn't stop until I was against the back of the couch—and then his finger started moving faster.

"You're going to make me come before I even get a chance to think about it." My mouth opened wide, and I felt my body shudder.

"You're going to come so many times tonight that you won't even remember your own damn name." He kissed my neck and nibbled my ear.

"Oh god..." My muscles tensed up, and I felt the pressure swelling inside me.

Bryant kissed his way down to my shoulder—then he pulled at my dress. His finger kept swirling around my clit and sending currents of euphoria through my entire body. I couldn't even think. I just let the pleasure take charge and drive me towards the pleasure I craved. The pressure began to release, and my knees buckled, but I fell against him. The orgasm made my body shake as the bliss released the endorphins into my veins.

He kept his finger moving until the orgasm faded, and then he began to remove my dress. I tried to unbutton his shirt, but my fingers were still shaking. My dress slid down my curves, and my bra was exposed—he kissed my breasts through the satin while he unfastened it. The instant my nipples were exposed, I felt his tongue on my right one—he kissed and caressed it until it was hard nub and then moved over to the left one. It got the same treatment, and the tingling sensation returned as the desire roared to life again.

"Has anyone ever tasted you?" Bryant lifted his head up and his eyes locked on mine.

"No." I shook my head back and forth and felt my pussy twinge as I imagined it.

"I think it's time for that to change." He took my hand and led me around to the front of the couch as my dress slid down a little more.

Bryant pulled me into his arms and finished sliding my dress to the floor. He pressed his lips to mine and our tongues intertwined as he pulled me down to the couch. His lips finally broke from mine and he teased my skin—then he slowly slid to the floor between my thighs. He pulled me forward, forced my legs apart, and let his tongue swirl against the sensitive flesh on the inside of my thighs.

The couch was so big that I was almost flat when I leaned back against the cushion. Bryant kept his tongue moving against my skin, and each sweltering kiss got closer to my pussy. I could feel the heat from his breath—feel the lust that was left behind from the pleasure he had already brought me—and then I felt his tongue on the lips that no man had tasted before. His tongue pushed them apart, and the tip penetrated my pussy. I sucked air into my lungs as he penetrated me, and then he started to kiss his way up to my clit. His fingers pushed the hood away, and then I felt an enormous sensation of pleasure as his tongue danced around the sensitive nerve endings.

"That feels amazing," I gasped, and my back arched against the couch.

Bryant's finger was intense, but his tongue was magical. It was like a whole new experience that I never imagined could feel so good. Other girls had talked about it—I listened and nodded along like I agreed, even though I had no idea if it was as good as they said. It was—and it was *way* better than they described. It made me float on a cloud of euphoria while the intensity of the pleasure made me writhe. Bryant held me in place while his tongue moved in quick circles around the hard knot that formed. The pressure built up so fast that it made my head spin—but I didn't want that feeling to end. It was almost better than the release his finger delivered—I wanted to feel it as long as possible before the orgasm came.

"Please don't stop—oh god, please—it feels so good!" I put my hand on his shoulder, and my arm started to shake.

No—not yet! Please, I'm not ready to come...

I might not have wanted the pleasure to end, but there was no way I could stop the storm that was ready to blow through me. The feeling was just too intense to stave off the inevitable. The pressure built and built until I was squirming so much Bryant had to actually force me to stay in position. My hips bucked against him. My nails dug into his shoulder. My breathing was so hurried that it got caught in my throat—along with moans. That forced me to gasp for air—and then the pressure released in the midst of the tornado that was making my desire spin inside my body.

"I'm coming—fuck..." My hips lifted up and bucked several times as the bliss ripped through my soul.

The orgasm was intense, but it didn't peak as fast as the others. It was like a slow build towards magnificence—followed by a peak that didn't immediately spiral towards the last throe of pleasure. I was wrong when I assumed that it felt better to experience it rather than come. The orgasm it brought was a whole different level of bliss. I ascended to another plane of existence where the pleasure became jagged and mesmerizing.

My eyes rolled back in my head, and my vision went black. I wasn't unconscious. My body just didn't know how to process any of the other senses. It was like I could *taste* the pleasure —*smell* the pleasure—*hear* the pleasure—and *see* pure euphoria while my body experienced it in a way that was impossible to imagine without actually living the moment with his tongue against my clit. I peaked for so long that everything inside me went numb when the orgasm finally began to fade.

"Oh, dear god," I exhaled sharply as my senses started to return to normal.

"Did you like that?" Bryant kissed my inner thighs and worked his way up my body before he dropped down beside me on the couch.

"Yes…" I nodded weakly and felt him pull me into his arms. "That was incredible."

It was still daylight—I could see the light through the window—but I was so exhausted from the orgasm that my eyelids didn't want to stay open. I finally let them close for a couple of minutes—and was awakened my Bryant's lips on my neck. I didn't think I would be able to come again. I wasn't sure I could even lift my arms. Bryant slowly caressed my skin with the tips of his fingers, and then followed every stroke with a light kiss.

His touch slowly pulled me back to reality—it made my breathing get heavier, and my pulse race. That gave me a second wind that I didn't expect, but I wasn't going to let it go to waste with another orgasm that would sap the remnants of strength I managed to find. It was time for Bryant to let me tease and torture him a little bit—that would give my body more time to recover before he took my innocence—and I had no doubt that he was going to do it before the night was over.

"I shouldn't be the only one naked." I bit down on my bottom lip and grinned as I started pulling on Bryant's tie while my fingers fumbled with the buttons on his shirt.

"I guess it's only fair." He put his hand the knotted part of his tie.

"No, I'll do it." I pushed his hand away. "You got to undress me—it's my turn."

"Okay." He smiled and let his hand fall away.

I knew Bryant had a gorgeous physique. I spent my teenage years trying to sneak a peek without gawking—I'm sure I gawked a time or two, but I did my best to be sly about it. I pulled his tie until it was loose; then kept tugging until it unraveled from his neck. I finally got to see his beautiful ink up close when I started unbuttoning his shirt. He leaned forward so I could strip it off. The sight of his muscular physique was enough to make my pussy get wetter—if that was possible—it definitely reacted with a tingle that made me shudder.

There were little details I never noticed when he swam in the pool while I was visiting or walked by without a shirt on. He had roses with thorns that started on his chest and curved into a vine on his left arm—I realized that the stem was colored to resemble a Picasso—chaotic designs that formed something beautiful when you saw it from a distance. I pressed my lips to his ink and started to trace it with my tongue. He let out a gasp and moved his hand to my thigh, but I immediately pushed it off.

"I already told you—it's my turn now." I smiled and moved my hand to his belt buckle.

"I can't even touch you?" he exhaled sharply.

"You've done enough of that already." I narrowed my eyes. "You'll get another turn once I make *you* come."

"Fuck…" His cock throbbed as soon as the words left my lips. "Okay—I'll try to keep my hands to myself."

I unbuckled Bryant's belt, unbuttoned his pants, and started to pull them down his hips. He lifted up enough for me to pull them down, and I reached for his boxers once his pants were around his knees. His cock got even more engorged once it was freed from the fabric prison. It was thick, hard, and practically pulsating with his desire. If it was as sensitive as my pussy, then I was definitely going to enjoy watching him get consumed with the same pleasure that he gave me. I let my fingernails drag against his inner thighs as I started kissing his chest again—I worked my way up to his neck—teased his earlobes—and then started moving down his abdomen.

I avoided his cock because I wanted to make him squirm a little bit before I made him come—but I found out just how sensitive his balls were when my nails lightly grazed against them. He let out a long sigh, and his muscles tightened up. It was similar to the reaction I had when he first started teasing me. I kissed his abdominal muscles—moved my lips lower—swirled my tongue against the skin right beside his cock and watched the way he reacted. He was definitely enjoying it, even if it wasn't what he truly wanted—yet.

Turning him on is a lot hotter than I expected—I just have to resist the desire to feel his touch until I make him come.

Chapter Eight

I had no idea what to expect when Taylor told me that she was a virgin. I tried to feel guilty about being her first, but I just couldn't find that emotion in the kaleidoscope of passion was already erupting between us. She wouldn't have been there unless she wanted to be—and I was honored that she wanted to give me her innocence. I had no idea what the relationship would become after we gave in to the insatiable hunger burning inside both of us. She had been a virgin for twenty-three years—I didn't think she would sleep with me unless there was *something* lingering beneath the surface that went deeper than lust—but it was really hard to think about that when I tasted her lips and felt her body pressed against me.

I certainly can't think about it right now—not when those lips keep getting closer and closer to my cock.

"God damn..." My head fell back against the couch when her tongue danced along my pelvis and started moving towards my balls. "That feels so fucking good."

I teased Taylor—I enjoyed it too. It was only fair that she returned the favor, even if I desperately wanted to feel her lips on my cock. I could tell by the look in her eyes that she knew *exactly* what she was doing when she started teasing me, even if she had never done it before. All of those seconds I spent kissing her inner thighs were returned in minutes that felt like hours while my dick throbbed.

It got to the point, I would have gotten down on both knees and begged for what I craved if she asked. I was normally pretty dominant in the bedroom, but I didn't feel that need with Taylor. Watching her discover my pleasure points was incredibly hot and knowing that I was the first man to feel those lips on my skin made my cock ache with desire.

"You're such a tease." I tried to keep a serious expression on my face, but all I could do was smile.

"Oh?" She bit down on her bottom lip. "Would a tease do this?"

Taylor wrapped her hand around my cock and leaned forward—then I felt her tongue on my balls. My whole body jerked forward and intense pleasure coursed through me. I couldn't respond to her question. My throat closed up, and the only thing that escaped it was a moan. Taylor circled my balls several times and covered them with her saliva—then her hand started to slowly move up and down my shaft. Her lips were soft, and her tongue was like velvet on my balls. It was the biggest tease ever, but the pleasure was so good that I didn't want to rush it. If she wanted to make me squirm before her lips even made it to my cock, then I was her willing victim— that enthusiasm was so damn hot it made my head spin.

"You didn't answer me." She pulled her tongue away from my balls. "I thought you would like that…"

"Oh god…" I exhaled sharply. "I really liked it—you don't have to stop."

"I thought you would prefer my tongue here…" She slid her hand to the base of my shaft and rolled her tongue around the head of my dick.

"Fuck." My body tensed up. "Don't stop doing that either."

"I've never had one in my mouth before." Taylor kissed the bottom of my shaft and licked her way back to the head.

"If you keep saying things like that, I'm going to come before you ever do." I balled my fists and quivered.

"You've made me come several times already..." She slid her tongue down to my balls and stroked my shaft several times before her tongue started massaging the bottom again.

"You're not done either—and if you tease me too much, I'll get my revenge before you get to come again." I flashed her the wickedest grin I could muster.

"I wouldn't want that..." She matched my wicked grin with one of her own—and kept eye contact as her mouth opened wide, so the head of my cock could slide across her lips.

Taylor's mouth was warm—wet—and felt incredible on my cock. Her inexperience showed as soon she tried to actually *do* what all of the teasing was leading to. She managed to get her lips around my shaft but struggled to create momentum. It was stop-go-adjust—and then try again. It felt good, and I didn't mind letting her experiment until she figured out how to do it. I moaned every time I felt her tongue massage the bottom— sighed when she slid down my shaft. After a few minutes of getting acclimated to having me in her mouth, she started to develop a rhythm and got the tight seal that turned a good feeling into one that made my whole body shudder while excitement built at a rapid pace.

"Yeah..." I exhaled sharply. "Just like that..."

Once Taylor figured out how to properly do it, her mouth turned into my personal paradise. She got enough saliva on my shaft to keep her lips moving, and they got faster as she got more comfortable with the motions. She took me deep into her throat—not far enough to swallow my entire cock, but enough to make it feel amazing. She kept trying to force it deeper, and

I heard a couple of gags, but she didn't stop. She kept getting close—feeling her *try* to swallow my cock was almost as good as having it buried in her throat. I finally put a hand on her head and gave her the nudge she needed once her throat relaxed—her lips slid down my shaft and touched my balls.

"Fuck." My hips jerked. "God damn, you're going to make come so hard…"

It would have been embarrassing to admit that I hadn't been with a woman since my wife left me. The closest I came to getting any action was when Alexis Devereaux approached me at the art show. Even after years of being without, I wouldn't have succumbed to her poisonous charm—but Taylor drew me in from the moment I laid eyes on her. Maybe it was some form of twisted destiny that pulled us together—or maybe I was just so far gone that I needed Taylor's innocence to show me how to *feel* again.

"Right there—oh god!" My body started to shake.

I felt my balls get tight—and then the pressure valve sent pre-cum into Taylor's mouth. I was afraid she would pull away when she tasted it—but she just moaned—then she pulled me deep into her throat and held my cock there as I started to erupt. The cum surged through my shaft, and then it exploded into her throat. She swallowed without missing a beat and bobbed her head a couple of times, which made more cum splatter into her mouth. She kept her lips moving and swallowed until every drop had been drained from my balls. My hand fell away from her head—I felt like I had died and went to heaven. I had almost forgotten how good it felt to have someone else make me come—I felt weak and energized at the same time.

"Damn, that was amazing." I exhaled sharply as Taylor removed her lips from my cock and climbed back onto the couch.

"How long will it be before you're ready to go again?" She slid closer to me. "That turned me on…"

"Give me a few minutes." I chuckled under my breath. "Then I'll take you to the bedroom."

"You're not going to take my virginity in the living room?" She pressed her lips to my arm. "I was just starting to like it down here."

"I think the bed will be more comfortable for both of us." I put a hand on her leg and slowly moved my fingers along her inner thigh.

"Are you going to start teasing me already?" She bit down on her bottom lip and grinned.

"Absolutely." I nodded.

Taylor's curves were so fucking gorgeous. She was so delicate and soft. I just wanted to lay beside her—I wanted the closeness of skin-on-skin. I wanted her in my arms and that want was turning into a need—every moment that we spent together heightened my desire for her. My thoughts were starting to toy with me—I was beginning to wonder if we could actually have a relationship—as inherently *wrong* as it would be.

Deep down, I knew that was practically impossible and unfair to her. I had already lived the years she had ahead of her. I had kids older than her—and I didn't know if I could give her a family if she wanted one. It was better to push those thoughts into the darkness where they belonged, because I didn't know if they could ever see the light of day.

"Are you ready to go upstairs?" I pressed my lips to Taylor's leg and slowly kissed my way towards her abdomen.

"If you are…" She leaned back and sighed.

"I'm ready." I looked down at my cock, which was slowly starting to engorge with more desire for the beautiful woman next to me.

"I think I remember which room is yours…" She leaned forward and started to stand.

"Do you?" I raised an eyebrow. "You've never been in it."

"Is that what you think?" She giggled and started walking towards the stairs—teasing me with a sway of her hips. "Obviously you don't know what goes on under your roof."

"I think you better explain…" I growled under my breath and started to stand.

"Catch me and I might tell you…" She scurried towards the stairs, and I took off in hot pursuit—she was a lot faster than me—I silently cursed myself for cutting back on my cardio workouts.

Lifting is a great way to work off some aggression—but it doesn't help much when I need to chase down a woman half my age.

Benson Estate was a maze to anyone who didn't know the layout—but Taylor had the advantage of knowing it almost as well as I did. I was curious to know how she knew which bedroom was mine—the kids weren't supposed to be in the east wing of the estate unless we were home, and guests *definitely* weren't allowed there. The main part of the estate was for entertaining, and I more or less let my kids take over the west wing as long as they cleaned up after themselves. My ex-wife usually picked up their slack when they didn't, which infuriated me at times, but I was always too busy with work to do anything about it.

"Okay—where the hell did you go?" I narrowed my eyes—it was getting dark, but I could see that she wasn't in my bedroom.

"Marco…" I heard giggling from one of the other rooms.

"Really?" I sighed and ran towards the room.

"Marco…" Her voice echoed from the hallway. "If you play along, you might actually find me."

"Fine…" I growled and shook my head. "Polo."

We played a hide-and-seek version of Marco Polo in the

east wing, and it became clear that Taylor knew that part of the estate better than she should have. Anyone who had been in the west wing could figure out the basic floor plan since they were identical, but I had made a few modifications that she breezed right through when I thought she would hit a dead end. I finally heard her calling me—and as I zeroed in on her voice, I realized that my bedroom door was open. I walked down the hall with a purpose and found her stretched out on my bed with a huge smile on her face.

"Marco..." She giggled and slid close to the edge of the bed.

"Polo." I walked over and crawled into bed. "You really do know which room is mine—you must have done a lot more *wandering around* than I realized when you visited..."

"I was curious." She looked up at me and shrugged. "It's a big house—it's not like I was going to *steal* anything."

"You were always a little more trustworthy than some of the others that visited." I nodded. "Still, you broke the rules..."

"Are you going to punish me?" She tried to make her voice whinier than normal—which sounded pretty comical. "Am I no longer welcome in your home, Mr. Benson should I put my clothes on and leave?"

"Oh, you're not going anywhere." I reached over and grabbed her wrist. "But I *am* going to give you a spanking."

"Wait!" She squirmed in my grasp as I rolled her over and put a little pressure on her back so that she couldn't move.

"Such a naughty girl..." I traced the back of her thighs and the curve of her ass. "You knew the rules."

"I did..." She sighed and stopped struggling when she felt my touch.

"You chose to break them." I moved my hand to the other side of her ass and traced down her thigh.

"I can't deny that." I felt goosebumps forming underneath my touch.

"Now I have to punish you." I pulled my finger away and cupped her ass.

"Fine—just one." She lifted her ass up against my hand.

"I think this deserves more than one." I teased her by sliding forward and gently stroking her pussy.

"Two?" She moaned and looked over her shoulder at me.

"I was thinking ten." I pulled my finger away.

"That's too many…" She shook her head and groaned. "I've never been spanked before."

"Well I certainly don't think you're going to learn your lesson with *two*." I narrowed my eyes and chuckled.

"Fine…" She groaned again—but there was a hint of playfulness, and she rubbed her ass against my hand. "Ten it is."

"That seems more appropriate." I lifted my hand and brought it down on the right side of her ass.

SMACK!

"That's one." She dropped her head and giggled.

"You don't have to count them." I pulled my hand back and gave her two quick ones—the second landed on the left side of her ass, and the other landed in the same spot as the first.

SMACK! SMACK!

"Ow…" She winced as the third one landed, but she wiggled her ass and pressed it against my hand.

"Are you beginning to learn your lesson, naughty girl?" I pulled my hand back.

SMACK! SMACK! SMACK!

"Maybe…" She exhaled sharply.

SMACK! SMACK! SMACK! SMACK!

"Now?" I let my hand stay where the last one landed.

"Yes—lesson learned!" She nodded quickly.

"Good, maybe we won't have to repeat this again." I leaned back and dropped down on my elbow beside her.

"I don't know." She rolled to the side and grinned. "That

kind of turned me on—I had no idea it would be so hot, having you spank me."

"You got off easy; it wasn't meant to hurt you." I brushed a stray hair away from her face. "Mainly because I want something else a whole lot more than I want to punish you for your naughty behavior."

"Oh yeah?" Hunger flashed in her eyes. "What's that?"

"I think you already know…" I put my hand on her hip and leaned forward to kiss her.

Our lips came together, and the passion was reignited in an instant. Taylor rolled over onto her back, and our lips stayed seared together as I mirrored her movement. My hands explored her body while her hands explored mine. My cock was fully engorged and ready—her pussy was practically dripping with desire. Every tease—every touch—it had all been building to the moment when her innocence would finally be mine.

I rubbed her pussy with my finger—pushed it inside her—and gave her a few gentle thrusts until I was against her hymen. She definitely wasn't lying about being a virgin—not that I thought she was. It wasn't the first time a virgin had graced my bed, but that was in high school—and I had no idea what I was doing. The years had given me some experience, so I knew that I would have to be gentle.

"I'm ready…" Taylor moved her lips to my ear, and she purred her words. "I want you to be my first."

"I'm going to take very good care of you tonight." I kissed her neck. "Just relax."

"I know you will." She nodded, and a smile spread across her face. "I trust you."

I just have to go slow—I want her first time to be special.

Chapter Nine

TAYLOR

$\mathscr{I}$ was so turned on that it felt like I was buzzing, despite not having a single sip of alcohol. I wasn't scared of losing my virginity, but the experience was still a mystery, and that left some lingering anxiety inside my head. Bryant erased that with his lips—he kissed my neck—teased my ears—and slowly pushed my legs apart as he positioned himself between them. I fantasized about him being the first man that took me to bed—but I never imagined that it could actually become reality.

"You're so beautiful..." Bryant let his lips linger on my neck, and I felt his cock against the entrance of my pussy. "It's been so long since I've felt anything—these few days with you have been amazing—and tonight is going to be even better."

"I want you..." I exhaled sharply as he began to penetrate me.

I would have never dared to even try when he was married —and even if he wasn't, my friendship with Victoria would have prevented it. Maybe there was a small part of me that had always compared the guys I met to the one who held a special place in my heart because he was my first crush—that seemed like a silly thought, but I never truly stopped wanting him—even after Victoria moved away and I stopped seeing him on a regular basis. All it took was a few seconds with him for those feelings to come back—and that set everything in motion for me to end up in his arms—which was exactly where I wanted to be.

"I'm going to go slow until you get used to it." Bryant lifted up and held the base of his cock as he began to push it deeper.

"Oh wow..." I grimaced when I felt the pain of being stretched for the very first time.

"It won't hurt for long." He leaned forward and silenced my impending groan with a kiss.

Bryant slowly pushed his dick into the entrance of my pussy and gave me a few gentle thrusts as he worked his way inside me. I knew the first time would be uncomfortable. I had heard enough girls talk about losing their virginity to expect it. Once the initial shock wore off, it wasn't as bad as I expected—until he was deep enough for his cock to make contact with my hymen. He made sure I was ready before he shattered the membrane with a harder thrust, and the sting was noticeable—even more so when he pushed past it.

When the pain got to be a little more than I thought I could handle, I simply stared into Bryant's eyes—that steel-blue stare used to enthrall me when I was younger, and that hadn't changed. He slowed the speed of his thrusts and didn't try to go deeper—it was like he could read my mind without me having to say anything at all. He gave me time to adjust to the way it felt—and the pleasure began to manifest in a different way. It was internal—a little more muted than it was when his tongue was against my clit—but it seemed to be a form of pleasure that tugged at my emotions while it made me tingle.

"That feels good..." I dug my nails into his shoulder. "Don't stop."

"It's not a matter of telling me to stop or keep going." He

leaned forward until his lips were against my ear. "I still haven't decided how many times I'm going to make you come before I do."

"Once?" I grimaced as he pushed a little deeper, but it didn't hurt as bad as it previously did.

"You need to set your expectations *much* higher," he growled into my ear.

"Twice?" I exhaled sharply when he pulled back and drove his cock past the point that had just gave me a twinge of pain.

"Still not high enough—I'm thinking *ten*." He gave me a harder thrust.

"Is ten the magic number with you for everything?" My head rolled back, and I felt a quick burst of pleasure.

"It's what I think you can handle…" He lifted up and put his hands on my thighs.

"Do the ones I already got count?" I bit down on my bottom lip and grinned.

"No." He narrowed his eyes. "Those were just a tease…"

I really don't think I can handle ten—the ones I got downstairs nearly destroyed me.

Bryant kept his hands on my thighs and started to deliver thrusts that were both quicker and harder than the previous ones. It was a mixture of discomfort and pleasure—sometimes it was hard to tell which feeling was stronger. He didn't have much further to go until every inch of his cock was buried inside me. I was ready for it—because I knew that would be the point where my body adjusted based on what I had felt so far.

It didn't hurt except when he went deep—aside from the spot where my hymen had stood for twenty-three years—that spot was still tender. My body was adjusting to Bryant—my pussy fit him like a glove once he introduced it to pleasure. I was so happy that my first time was with a man who was experienced enough to take care of me—it was definitely worth the wait.

"You feel so fucking good," Bryant exhaled sharply, and I started to see real pleasure register on his face—there were hints of it before, but it was getting more intense.

"So, do you…" I sighed, and a moan rushed across my lips. *That isn't a lie—every thrust is getting better than the one before it.*

Bryant gave me a few quick thrusts, then he squeezed my thighs, shifted his weight, and the last few inches disappeared into my pussy. I grimaced—but the pain evaporated quickly. He left his cock buried inside me until I adjusted, and then he gave me a few gentle thrusts. Those felt *really* good. He pulled back to the entrance of my pussy and gave me the slowest thrust imaginable, but I got every inch of his length before he repeated that motion. It was a tease, but a damn good one. He started to alternate—a few gentle thrusts—a harder one—then the extremely slow thrust. The pleasure was incredible—I couldn't figure out which thrusts I liked best because they all felt amazing in a different way.

"It's not going to take much to make me come." A loud moan echoed in my throat.

"I'm going to teach you how to come on command—and you're going to *love* it." He narrowed his eyes and chuckled.

"Oh god…" I felt the familiar pressure building.

Bryant kept repeating the same rhythmic thrusts as the pressure continued to build. The harder thrusts got me close, the slower ones pulled me back from the edge, and the slowest one made my whole body quiver when it went deep. I was ready to come, and he could have easily brought the orgasm to the surface with a steady stream of harder thrusts, but he seemed to like toying with me. The pressure got so intense that I could feel my muscles getting tight—but I wasn't there yet. He kept me on the edge for what felt like an eternity before the slower thrusts were enough to make the pressure build—then the slowest one sent me spiraling into euphoria. As soon as he felt my pussy spasm, he picked up the speed—

and the quick thrusts tore my understanding of pleasure in half.

"I'm gonna come! Oh god! Fuck!" My mouth opened wide, and my words just turned into garbled nonsense as my body erupted in bliss.

Bryant bent me to his will—and I didn't realize he was doing it until my body was already at his mercy. Once the orgasm seized control, he literally owned it. He used the quick thrusts to make it peak so high my entire body shook—then gave me some slower ones to keep that peak going—but it wasn't just moving in a straight line—the peak was getting higher too. Another series of harder thrusts made my body literally convulse, and a stronger orgasm devoured the first one. It was a high that I couldn't come down from—and it was still trying to peak, despite the fact that I had already been taken to a level that I didn't even realize could exist.

"Come for me again." He leaned forward, and his words came out as a raspy-growl. "I want to feel it—and you're going to do what I say."

"I…" I tried to say *can't*, but that word didn't exist in my vocabulary—nor was it true—because my body simply obeyed him.

In the midst of orgasmic euphoria, I felt a stronger sensation emerge. I heard stories about the mythical g-spot but had no idea if they were true until Bryant awakened it. It roared to life with another orgasm on top of the newfound source of bliss. I was starting to lose count—and I began to actually believe he could make me come ten times—but there was no way I would know for sure. My thoughts were shattered, and my head was spinning out of control. It was filled with so many endorphins I didn't know how to function—all I knew how to do was come on command.

"You're not done," Bryant growled into my ear.

I know…

Bryant started to hammer his cock into my g-spot. The orgasm that was currently consuming me—whichever one it was—began to fade. That was a moment of respite that I savored in the midst of passion, but I could feel another one coming. All of my senses faded except the pleasure I felt when the next powerful surge of euphoria swept through my veins. My pussy had gotten so sensitive that it was beginning to ache from the spasms, but the pleasure was too intense to focus on anything else. I couldn't even tell when one orgasm stopped and another one began—I didn't know if he could tell either. I was just strung out on the endorphins while my body chased the next high, they would bring.

"Now you're going to make *me* come." Bryan pushed my chin to the side and kissed my neck—slowly lifting his lips to my ear.

"Yes—I want to feel you…" I dug my nails into his back.

Bryant's cock had throbbed several times while he yanked the bliss from within me, but it started to pulsate even harder than it did when I used my mouth to make him explode. Feeling it throb and pulsate against my g-spot was enough to bring me close to the edge—if it was ten, he was right on target—it definitely wasn't less. His thrusts got faster—harder —and I could hear the bed protesting underneath us. A loud primal roar echoed in his throat—his head flew back—and then I felt him come. His seed flooded my pussy—quick, powerful bursts that teased me before a gasp of pleasure caused a release that sent me across the threshold of euphoria one final time. My spasms milked his cock as he unloaded inside me, and when the final drop was drained from his balls, he simply slumped forward.

"Give me a few minutes—then I'll be ready to go again." His voice sounded dry and raspy—like the release had taken everything out of him.

"Again?" I sighed. "My whole body feels numb…"

"It'll pass." He pressed his lips to my ear. "Because you belong to me now—and you're going to come every time that I tell you to."

I promised myself it would only be once—I don't know if I'll be able to keep that promise now…

Several hours later

I wanted to stay in Bryant's arms until the sun came up, but I knew it wasn't a good idea. I was old enough to come home when I wanted, but I had never stayed out all night—my mother would definitely worry. Bryant kept his word—it wasn't long until he was ready for another round of mind-bending bliss. Thankfully, it was just a quick trip to paradise for us both to get one final release. I don't think I could have handled more than that. We stayed tangled in a lover's embrace for a few hours after—we both dozed just to get enough energy to crawl out of bed. He drove me home— we shared one last kiss when he stopped in front of my house —and then I had to sneak in under the cover of darkness for the first time since high school.

At least everyone is asleep…

"You're getting home pretty late." A light came on at the end of the hall, and I nearly jumped out of my heels when I saw Anna standing in her doorway.

Scratch that—apparently my sister isn't in bed.

"Keep your voice down." I brought my finger to my lips to shush her. "I don't want mom to wake up."

"You must have a boyfriend." A devilish grin spread across her face, but she did lower her voice to a whisper.

"Don't say anything." I shook my head back and forth. "Please…"

"I won't." She smirked and chuckled. "I just hope I'm not still sneaking in the house when I'm twenty-three…"

Hopefully the guy you're with won't be someone that can't come to the front door. Wait—still?

I didn't get a chance to grill my sister about what she said —and truthfully, I was too exhausted. It wasn't my place anyway. I remembered how I was at sixteen, and while I was a fairly good kid, I made a few mistakes that turned into great memories. I was just surprised to hear that she had possibly done something in the evening hours except stay up late reading whatever book she had her nose buried in—I didn't think she even had a social life. She was smart enough not to do anything stupid—smarter than I was at her age.

She's probably smarter than I am right now. I don't regret what I did with Bryant, but if this continues, we're not going to be able to hide it forever…

Chapter Ten

BRYANT

The next day

The scent of passion and desire still lingered in my bedroom and on the sheets when I woke up the next morning. I wished I had awakened to the sight of Taylor's beautiful body beside me, but I understood why she couldn't stay. I was so exhausted from what we shared that I didn't even bothering working out before I went to work. I showered, got dressed like a zombie going through the motions, and fixed a cup of coffee before I walked out the door. I normally waited until I got to the office to have my first dose of caffeine, but I didn't think I would be able to make it there without having some to get my blood pumping.

It's going to be a busy day too, because I put off some of my meetings yesterday to see if I could figure out what is going on with Alexis Devereaux.

Cassie was as chipper as ever, but I needed more coffee before I was ready for it, so I tried to just shut her out as I walked to my office. I did take a moment to compliment her new haircut, because she would have been in a foul mood if I didn't—that was a mistake I only made once. My morning was consumed with meetings that took way too long. They were pointless for the most part—the economy was in good shape which made my job easier. It was the downturn that usually required attention—or an emergency like we had the previous weekend. By lunch, I was feeling ragged—it was the first time I had felt my age in a long time—and I didn't like it. I silently swore to put in a little more cardio at the gym—I was going to need it if I intended to keep up with the voracious appetite I awakened in Taylor.

"Hey, Mr. Benson." Cassie pushed my door open. "I'm about to take my lunch break. Do you want me to pick something up for you?"

"No—wait." I held up my hand. "Actually, yes. I need to work through lunch."

"Yep, I'm going to the sandwich shop—BLT, right?" She raised an eyebrow. "Heavy on the mayo."

"That's right." I nodded.

Bacon and extra mayonnaise aren't the best way to kick off my new dedication to extra cardio but fuck it.

"Oh, and you got a call from Moretti's. They said you had a reservation last night, but you didn't show up?" She titled her head inquisitively.

"Right…" I sighed. "Please apologize—actually, you know what—order lunch from them for the entire office on Friday. That should smooth things over."

"And make everyone here very happy." Cassie beamed. "Myself, included!"

"Perfect." I reached for my coffee and nodded.

I found myself spacing out as I tried to do work, but it wasn't aimless. I was thinking about Taylor—and wishing that I didn't have to wait until the weekend to see her again. I tried everything except tying her to the bed to convince her that she needed to be back in my arms when the sun went down, but she had a few assignments for school that required her attention. She promised to make it up to me once we were together again—so I reluctantly agreed to wait—but that didn't mean I couldn't daydream about her between meetings, even if I did have emails that required my attention. I barely got anything done during the time I reserved for lunch, despite staying in the office for that very reason.

Damn it; Cassie rescheduled one of the meetings I canceled yesterday for four-thirty, and it's with Jon Alcott—I already know that's going to take a while because he needs to talk through some post-divorce options for his investments...

I drank coffee with my lunch, drank another cup as soon as I was done, and by the afternoon, I was starting to feel somewhat normal again. The crash was going to be a bad one, so it was probably best that I wasn't spending the night with Taylor. I would have pushed myself past my limits just to savor the passion, but I would have really been feeling it the next day. There was a time when I could *go* for several days without needing much sleep, but I think the sleepless nights I experienced after Shaina was born changed my constitution—or maybe I just needed to accept the fact I was forty-five.

I didn't feel forty-five last night—fuck, Taylor made me feel like a teenager again.

"Mr. Benson?" Cassie pushed my door open. "Mr. Alcott is early..."

"That's okay." I looked up at her and nodded. "Send him in."

Maybe I'll get home earlier than I hoped...

"Ah, there's the busiest man in Carson Cove." Jon walked into my office and waved his hands towards me.

"Most days," I chuckled under my breath and stood. "Would you like a drink?"

"Yes, please—you might as well make it a double." The

smile quickly faded from his face—it probably took a lot for him to wear it into my office.

"Absolutely." I walked to the small bar I kept in my office for clients and poured him a glass of whiskey—double, just like he requested. "I had a few of my guys run some figures for you. I think you'll be okay—your company is doing great."

"Mary wants me to sell it…" he exhaled sharply.

"Wait, what?" My eyes opened wide, and I nearly spilled his drink when I tried to put it down on my desk. "That's your father's company!"

"It's an asset—according to my divorce attorney—and assets can be liquidated in a divorce if the compensation package requires it." John grabbed his drink and took a huge gulp.

"That's ridiculous." I sat down behind my desk with a thud. "Mary wouldn't do that to you—would she?"

"I don't even know anymore." He shrugged and a long sigh passed across his lips. "We originally agreed to use the same attorney and make things amicable. Yesterday, she mentioned that she didn't know if our assets could be split fairly unless I sold Alcott Inc.—that caused a huge fight, as you can probably imagine. She packed a bag and left—two hours later, I got a call from my attorney—Mary fired him and hired Drake Barnes."

"Fuck man, he's a damn snake." I gritted my teeth. "He's unethical as hell—he almost got *disbarred* a few years ago."

"That's what worries me." Jon took another drink of his whiskey. "I can't help but wonder if Mary had already talked to him before we had our fight—she's never been involved in the company at all. The package that our attorney was putting together was very fair in my opinion with alimony that would hurt every month, but I was willing to pay it. Drake Barnes sent something to my attorney earlier today officially with-drawing from that agreement—on the grounds that the future earnings of Alcott Inc. weren't properly estimated. It's bullshit."

"Yes, it is." I nodded in agreement. "There won't be any future earning if you have to sell Alcott Inc."

"That's his point." Jon shook his head angrily. "I could tank the company and screw Mary out of what she's owed—selling it now avoids that."

"It sounds like you may have to go to trial just sort out the bullshit." I sighed and leaned forward. "Now, *I* need a drink."

"You were lucky, Bryant. Your divorce was smooth—I thought mine would be too." Jon downed the rest of his whiskey and held out his glass for more.

I never considered myself lucky when I watched the love of my life walk out of it—but at least I kept Benson Enterprises.

"We may need to reschedule this meeting." I filled his glass and poured a drink for myself. "I based everything on the old agreement you sent me—this will change things."

"Yeah, I know." He nodded. "I just needed someone to talk to."

"Then maybe we should find somewhere to drink with a better atmosphere than an office building…" I put my drink down on the edge of my desk.

"Chateau Prime?" Jon raised an eyebrow. "Good memories at that place—I could use a few."

"Sure," I chuckled under my breath. "I'll drive."

Chateau Prime was an upscale den for gentlemanly debauchery. It was the kind of place fathers took their sons when they were old enough to be considered *men*—and not just because of their age—it was a rite of passage that was as old as Carson Cove itself. I never got that experience with my own father—he promised to take me the day that I became an officer in the company, but I had to skip that stage of my career entirely when I was forced to take over as CEO. Instead,

I went with Jon—because if losing my father didn't make me a man, nothing else ever would.

Truthfully, I didn't have any fond memories of Chateau Prime. It was generally just a place for the happily married to congregate at the behest of their wives who scolded them when they got home with cigar smoke on their clothes and liquor on their breath—or any combination of the two. The waitresses always paraded around in skimpy little upscale dresses that were enough to draw a few eyes while maintaining a slight semblance of class. There were rumors that some *real* debauchery went on behind the scenes if you were willing to pay, but I sure as hell didn't want any of that—even when I was at my lowest point.

"Are you still dodging Alexis like the plague?" Jon looked over at me once we were seated in my car.

"Absolutely." I nodded quickly.

"I guess I would be too—if I had a hot new girlfriend. You going to tell me about her?" He narrowed his eyes.

"You saw that, huh?" I chuckled under my breath.

"I saw her send Alexis running for the door—Mary actually cracked a smile at that—probably the last one I'll ever see," he sighed. "So, what's her name—and does she have a sister?"

"Her name is Taylor and she's not my girlfriend—just a friend." I shook my head back and forth. "I believe her sister would be a little too young for you."

"Damn…" He shrugged. "Oh well, I guess I should wait until I actually sign my divorce papers before I start planning my next one."

"You've still got a few more to go before you're in Alexis Devereaux territory. Maybe you'll find the right woman next time." I nodded—and realized I was actually giving him advice I never took myself—until Taylor unexpectedly walked into my life.

We arrived at Chateau Prime, and the atmosphere was the same as I remembered—but that was better than drinking at my office, and I had a feeling that Jon needed to tie one on. We found a corner booth, and I let him rant while I provided a friendly ear—he finished three drinks before I was halfway through my first, so it was clear that he was going to be blackout drunk before we left. I had a few of those nights when I got divorced, so I understood—thankfully, I had so many responsibilities that I didn't get to linger in the bottle for long. I had no idea what I would have done if I lost Benson Enterprises when my wife decided to leave me—that would have turned the darkest point in my life into a literal nightmare.

"I just don't get it man," he sighed. "Alcott Inc. isn't going under. The company is in great shape. It's a cash-out-now option that just hurts everyone—god, what if Sawyer King tries to buy the company? What the fuck would I do then? How would I look all of my employees in the eye and tell them they're on the short route to an early retirement—without financial security."

"Yeah, it's a shitty situation." I nodded. "The only good thing is that Sawyer King seems to have left Carson Cove—so maybe someone will buy it that has the company's best interest in mind…"

"I sure as fuck hope so." He lifted his glass and took a drink —then finished it.

Jon's words got slurred, but he kept drinking—and before long he was talking about our high school years. He seemed to remember them with rose-colored glasses, but that was probably because they seemed better than what was dealing with at the moment. We definitely had fun in high school, but we were just dumb kids doing stupid things. I was curious to know where Jon's kids were—if they left with Mary or if their grandparents were watching them. I was afraid to bring anything up that he didn't want to discuss—it was risky since he was wound up about everything already.

"Bryant Benson, holy shit." A voice laced with a Cajun accent echoed from across the room, and I looked over to see a man approaching.

Fuck me, it's Danny Fontenot. What is this, a high school reunion? I thought he moved back to Louisiana.

"Danny?" Jon narrowed his eyes and then hopped to his feet. "Danny!"

Apparently, he's happier to see that bastard than I am—or maybe he's just so drunk he forgot what an asshole he is.

"Hey Danny." I gave him a nod while Jon decided to just go for a fucking hug.

"What are you two doin' at Chateau Prime? Hell, ain't seen either one of ya in years." Danny hugged Jon and then decided to sit down at our table without asking for an invitation.

"Us?" I raised an eyebrow. "I thought you left Carson Cove after college…"

"Naw, I been back a few years." He nodded. "My boys—got twins—they're tearing up the field at our old stompin' ground. Hell, that quarterback they got comin' up is supposed to have a cannon—might go to state—might break all our old records."

"Damn, they haven't been broken yet?" I raised my eyebrows in surprise.

"Naw man, we was legends—still are." He laughed and raised his beer to motion for the waitress to bring him another.

"Hell yeah, man." Jon leaned over and gave Danny a nudge. "Danny Fontenot! I can't believe it. What are you doing with yourself these days?"

Danny told us his life story—I tuned out and just stared at my drink, but I was forced to still hear most of it. Jon was having a good time and wasn't wallowing in his despair, so that was an improvement. Danny wasn't one of the so-called privileged in Carson Cove when I knew him. He was just a kid from the suburbs that could sniff out a quarterback's next play before they even figured it out themselves. He got a scholarship to LSU, which was where his family was from—knocked heads for another four years before he finally hung up his cleats. His financial situation had apparently changed for the better—but he didn't elaborate on it.

"Oh, ya two will never guess who I ran into the other day." He leaned forward and grinned. "Hot-ass Alexis."

"Yeah, never would have guessed you'd run into her in Carson Cove." I couldn't even hide the sarcasm in my voice.

"I don't want to sound like a playboy or anythin'—cause I love my wife—but I think she was hittin' on me." He grinned from ear-to-ear.

What the fuck is going on with her? Is she really that fucking desperate?

Jon decided that he needed to tell his own story about Alexis to match the one that Danny told, so I got to relive the events of the art show from Jon's perspective—which included a mention of Taylor. That, of course, meant Danny had to ask about my ex-wife—and Jon's soon to be ex—which soured Jon's temporary moment of joviality reliving our high school days. It seemed like the air got sucked out of the room after that, and it didn't take Danny long to look for an excuse to leave. I was glad to see him go—and it was about time for me to get Jon home before I literally had to carry him out of Chateau Prime.

"Are you about ready for me to drive you home?" I finished the drink I had been nursing most of the night and put the empty glass down.

"Yeah." Jon nodded and sighed. "I wanted to drink and forget all this shit—now I'm thinking about it all over again."

"Sorry…" I stood and motioned for him to follow me.

The drive to Jon's neighborhood was a somber one. He

knew he was going home to an empty house, and I fully under-stood how miserable that could be. The alcohol helped his mood while he was happy, but as soon as he got a vicious reminder of Mary, he was worse than he was before he took his first drink. I decided not to just drop him off—I followed him into the house and kept him company until he finally passed out. It was late, and my plan to go to bed early was definitely shot, but I knew I would sleep hard when I got there. I drove to my house, changed into a pair of shorts, and decided to check in with Taylor before I crashed. It might have been late for me, but I doubted she was in bed—not if she kept the kind of hours I did when I was in college—granted, I was usually up to no good instead of hitting the books.

Bryant: I missed you today…

Taylor: Hey! I was hoping I would hear from you before I went to sleep. I missed you too.

Bryant: I really have to wait until Saturday to see you?

Taylor: If you wait until Saturday, I can spend the whole day with you. Otherwise, I'll have to go home early to work on my school stuff.

Bryant: Okay, I guess that does sound better. I wish you could spend all night with me too…

Taylor: I probably could, but then I'd have to tell my mom why I'm not coming home. I'd like to avoid that conversation for now.

Bryant: Does that mean you plan to have it with her at some point?

Taylor: I don't like hiding it, but…

Bryant: I know. It's complicated.

Taylor: Can we just take it one day at a time for now?

Bryant: Of course.

Taylor: Thank you.

Bryant: I'm about to go to bed. I'm a little worn out…

Taylor: I wonder why—maybe the same reason I couldn't walk straight this morning?

Bryant: I wish I could have seen that.

Taylor: It wasn't flattering!

Bryant: I would have laughed.
Taylor: I would have thrown something at you!
Bryant: So violent...
Taylor: Goodnight :)
Bryant: Goodnight...

I couldn't help but smile as I climbed into bed—mainly because Taylor was going to be there beside me in a couple of days. As soon as I tried to go to sleep, my mind flashed back to what Danny said to us at Chateau Prime—which made me think of Alexis—the last person I wanted to be thinking about while I was lying in bed. There was definitely something going on with her that wasn't totally transparent. I wanted to just forget about her and accept that it wasn't my problem, but I felt like there was a reason she set her sights on me—I had trouble believing it was totally driven by greed. I wasn't entirely convinced that she was hitting on Danny—he was happily married and there was no way that fit into her game plan if what Taylor overhead was true.

There has to be something I'm missing... Fuck it. I've wasted enough time trying to figure her out—there's not a damn thing she can do to me right now because I sure as hell have no intentions of marrying her.

Chapter Eleven

TAYLOR

The next day

I woke up feeling rather refreshed. My muscles didn't ache when I got out of bed, which was a huge improvement over the previous day, and I got enough sleep not to feel like the staggering dead. I even got up early enough to beat Anna to the shower, and I was downstairs with a cup of coffee in my hand when I heard the shower start again. Our mother was always the first one up, but it took her longer to get ready. I sat down at the kitchen table and flipped through the assignments I had been working on—I always liked to proofread them in the morning after I had some time to let the information settle in my head a little bit. I didn't see any glaring errors, so I was rather relieved. My mother came charging down the stairs with a purpose, but she came to an abrupt stop when she got to the kitchen.

"You're up—and you made coffee." She looked at me and smiled. "Thank you."

"No problem." I nodded. "I wanted to look over my assignments before school."

"I thought you would be sleeping as long as you could—especially with the late hour you got in a couple nights ago." She poured a cup of coffee and eyed me suspiciously.

"Mom…" I looked down and sighed.

"I know, you're twenty-three now. You don't have to give me the song and dance. I'm not judging." She sat down across from me. "So, what's his name?"

Straight to the point—I should be used to that by now.

"It's really nothing." I shook my head back and forth. "It's all school-related."

There goes a lie—but I don't know how to tell the truth about Bryant. It's way too complicated for the kitchen table—or anywhere.

"Okay…" She nodded, but the suspicious stare didn't fade. "Well if you need to talk, I was twenty-three once too—and if you *are* dating, maybe we can compare notes, because…"

"Mom!" My head snapped back in surprise.

"I should get to work." She looked at her watch. "Have a good day. Please make sure your sister gets out the door on time."

"Will do, I love you, Mom." I sipped my coffee and smiled.

"Love you too." She made a quick dash for the door.

I hated lying to my mother but telling her the truth about Bryant seemed more devastating than a little white lie. I definitely didn't want to compare notes about our love life and hear about Dave or Steve, or whoever she was dating. I assumed it wasn't *that* serious since she hadn't introduced him to us yet. I did miss the closeness we used to have before my father left—just like I missed the connection I used to have with my little sister. My world revolved around art—and my mother's love of it faded after the divorce—my sister never cared about it to begin with. I felt guilty trying to talk about the stuff I was studying in school—I didn't even mention the art show to my mother. I knew that would make her think about my father, and all of the family vacations we used to plan around art exhibits.

"Good morning." Anna walked into the kitchen and immediately started making a bowl of cereal. "Mom is already gone?"

"Yeah, she just left." I sipped my coffee and nodded.

"Cool." She sat down across from me. "Why are you up so early? You usually don't make it downstairs before we leave."

"I just woke up a little earlier this morning." I shrugged.

"That's probably because you weren't sneaking in the house after midnight." She grinned and winked at me.

"Yeah, but it sounds like I might not be the only one…" I narrowed my eyes.

"I've only missed curfew a couple of times." She looked down, and I saw her blush—I hadn't seen her blush in years.

She definitely has a boyfriend—or someone that she's spending time with.

"Well, if you want to talk about it…" I let my words trail off as soon as I realized I was about to give her the same speech I avoided having with my mother.

"Nope." Anna shook her head back and forth. "Okay, I need to go to school."

"You haven't even finished your cereal." I raised an eyebrow.

"No time—see you tonight." She grabbed her books and waved as she walked to the door.

All three of us are dating someone right now, and nobody wants to talk about it—maybe Mom does, but Anna and I aren't really up for that discussion…

Later that day

"*H*ey, Taylor!" One of my friends at school, Melanie, waved at me as I was walking to my next class.

"Hey there, Mel." I acknowledged her and smiled as she approached. "It feels like I haven't seen you in weeks…"

"That does tend to happen when you switch majors." She laughed under her breath.

"How are things going in the Business Management world?" I raised an eyebrow.

"A little more promising than they were in the Art world." She shrugged. "I already have a couple of job offers—Alcott Inc. is hiring."

"Oh wow, I've heard good things about them." I nodded.

Being an art major doesn't exactly bring the job offers to you—maybe I should start looking so that I don't spend months trying to find something after graduation.

"We should hang out and catch up. It's been a while…" She shifted as a couple of students came walking by at a hurried pace. "Are you doing anything after school?"

"Just working on my assignments." I nodded. "Like every other day."

"Want to go stare at cute guys with me?" She batted her eyelashes.

"What do you mean?" I tilted my head inquisitively.

"Carson Cove University is hosting the local high school's football team—you know, they do that scrimmage game every year, and the coaches get to see how the guys they want to recruit do under pressure." She gave me a nudge. "Very few people go, so we can see some hot, sweaty guys in action—up close."

"Um…" I wrinkled my nose—I didn't want to just turn her down, but I wasn't really a fan of football.

"Come on; it'll be fun." She gave me another nudge. "If

it's boring, we can leave early and go get a drink or something."

"Okay." I nodded. "Sure."

Hopefully it'll be as boring to her as it will be to me.

I attended the scrimmage game she mentioned once when I was in high school, and again during my freshman year of college—mainly because I still had a few friends at Carson Cove High. If it was anything like the two games I had previously watched, it was just an excuse for the college guys to massacre the high school team. Truthfully, it was usually one of the only games Carson Cove University's football team won each year—my alma mater wasn't exactly known for its football program. The kids that were good went to colleges that actually won games. Still, as bored as I was by football, it would be good to hang out with Melanie. I didn't have that many friends at college, and we were a lot closer when we had classes together.

Later that day

$\mathcal{I}$ met Melanie after my last class, and we walked down to the football field. She was right—there weren't many people there. The audience mostly consisted of high school parents that were there to watch their kids get crushed by the college team, and a few students spread out across the bleachers—I assumed they were bored like us. Melanie and I were able to get seats near the fifty-yard line, which would allow her to get an eyeful of hot, sweaty guys in action—just like she wanted. I just hoped that she wouldn't want to stay long so that we could go and do something else. A drink would be nice—and it would be easier to catch up somewhere that was quieter.

"I would *so* date him—or him." Melanie motioned to a couple of football players that walked by without their helmets on.

"Still no luck in that department?" I raised an eyebrow.

"No, how about you?" She looked over at me.

"Maybe…" I looked down. "I'm seeing someone."

I guess there's no harm in telling Melanie that—it isn't like she's going to talk to anyone that shouldn't know.

"What?" Her eyes opened wide. "Is it someone that goes to school here?"

"Nah, he's—not in college." I smiled and decided that was as much information as I wanted to share.

"Anyone I know." She nudged me.

"I don't think so." I shook my head back and forth. "I don't even know if it's serious yet."

Or how long it'll be before I finally have to break it off with him—it certainly can't last forever.

Melanie didn't ask any more details—because the game started, and she got absorbed by the action. I'm not sure you could really call it *action*, per se. It was the Stone Devils of Carson Cove University taking on the Tigers of Carson Cove High—and the tigers just looked like kittens as the Stone Devils marched down the field to score a touchdown on the opening drive. The Tigers got the ball and lost it to a turnover—then the Stone Devils scored again. I was definitely bored. Melanie seemed to enjoy the bloodbath. The Tigers got the ball again, and the quarterback handed it to the running back. I was scared to watch him get mauled when the much larger players from my university went after him—but he took off like the wind.

"Bolt! Yes! Go!" A familiar voice echoed from the bleachers across the field, and I put my hand over my eyes to make sure I wasn't hearing things.

"Anna?" I blinked in confusion.

"Huh?" Melanie looked over at me.

"That's—my sister." I stared with a perplexed look on my face.

Anna ran down the bleachers as the guy she called Bolt made a dash for the end zone, and he definitely didn't look like a kitten. The back of his uniform said his last name was Bolton, a few people yelled out Gavin, and I quickly figured out how he got his nickname. He left the Stone Devils gasping for air as he blew them away with a speed that was almost unnatural.

The Tigers scored, and Bolt did a little dance in the end zone—then he walked to the fence and—*kissed* my little sister. It wasn't a passionate kiss—more like a peck—but she was smiling from ear-to-ear when he ran to join his teammates on the sideline. I hadn't seen a smile like that on her face since before my parents got divorced. That touchdown changed the momentum of the game a little bit and one thing was for sure —Bolt was a star. The quarterback had a good arm, but the Stone Devils didn't give him a chance to use it very often—Bolt did most of the heavy lifting.

"So, that's your sister over there—the one that keeps running to the fence every time the running back gets to the end zone." Melanie raised an eyebrow inquisitively.

"Yeah…" I nodded. "I had no idea she was dating a football player—I thought she was dating *someone*, but—wow."

"I hope she isn't in love," Melanie sighed. "A guy that good won't be hanging around Carson Cove after he graduates. He'll have offers from schools all over the country."

"That's probably true." I nodded. "Hopefully she's smart enough to realize that."

"Were you? At her age?" Melanie shook her head and laughed.

"I didn't have that problem when I was her age…" I looked back towards the field.

I'm not even smart enough to avoid it now. I know my relationship with Bryant can't last forever—and I keep letting myself fall for him a little more every single day.

The Tigers put up a good fight, but even a running back that could blow the Stone Devils away couldn't secure the game for them. The high school coach pulled his best players out after halftime when it was clear that they weren't going to win and some of his younger players got some experience being run over by the much larger guys from Carson Cove University.

Melanie decided that she didn't want to watch the massacre any longer after that, so we agreed to meet up at a restaurant downtown for dinner and drinks. I really needed to be working on stuff for school, but I hadn't spent much time with Melanie since she switched majors, so I decided that dinner out wouldn't set me back too much. It was a short drive from the university to the restaurant that she picked out.

I'd rather spend the time with Bryant, but we'll have Saturday...

"What do you want to drink? I think I want a margarita..." Melanie skimmed the drink menu as soon as we were seated at our table.

"Hmm." I picked up my menu. "I might just go with a glass of wine—oh wait, that's the price for one glass? I'll just have a margarita too..."

"I might need to talk to your sister." Melanie looked up from the menu and grinned. "I should get that Bolt guy's autograph before he ends up in the NFL."

"We thought one of the guys I went to high school was on the fast track to the NFL too..." I shrugged. "He looked really good against the local schools but ended up getting cut from the team when he made it to college—Bolt might not be that impressive against better players."

"Ah, I guess that makes sense." She nodded. "Big fish in a

little pond—or a very *rich* pond when it comes to Carson Cove."

"The land of the *privileged*," I chuckled under my breath.

"Yeah, if I don't land this job at Alcott Inc., I might have to head back into the real world when I graduate from college. Are you still planning to leave Carson Cove as soon as you get your degree?" She raised her eyebrows inquisitively.

"Honestly? I don't know…" I sighed. "There are some jobs local—graphic design and stuff like that."

"Are you still painting?" She tilted her head inquisitively.

I didn't get a chance to answer her question immediately, because the waiter came to take our order. We both ordered margaritas, smiled when he asked to see our ID, and then picked out an appetizer. We knew what we wanted to eat as well, so we saved him another trip to the table, and ordered that too. I decided to go with grilled chicken and steamed broccoli. Melanie was feeling a little more adventurous, so she got the chicken tenders and fries.

"Yeah, so—painting…" I looked down at the table. "I honestly haven't had much time to do paint lately. I enjoy it, but it's not like I'll ever make a living selling my work—I used to love showing them to my dad, but after he left—I don't know. Mom lost her love for art after the divorce and my sister just thinks it's dumb."

"You don't see your dad anymore?" She leaned back and winced. "I was always scared to ask because you talk about him in the past tense."

"I've seen him a couple of times." I shook my head and sighed. "He lives in the city now, and I think he has a new girlfriend that he's scared to introduce…"

I was interrupted again by our drinks and a promise that the appetizer would be there soon. Melanie didn't ask anything else about my dad, and I was thankful that she dropped the subject. It was still tough for me, but tougher on my mother, and toughest on my sister—I seemed to be the strong one, despite the connection I had with him when I was younger. I couldn't control his midlife crisis, and I preferred him to be happy than miserable with us. I just hoped that I could be a part of his new life one day, and I knew Anna would love to see him more. If both of my parents had moved on and were dating other people, there was no reason that we couldn't build a new family dynamic, even if it wasn't perfect.

"Oh god—I think this place is about to get busier." Melanie looked towards the door.

"Why?" I turned and saw several members of the Carson Cove High football team standing near the entrance. "They must be here to celebrate the fact that they didn't die on the field today…"

"There's your sister, holding hands with that Bolt guy." Melanie motioned towards the group.

"Wow…" I shook my head back and forth. " I'm beginning to think she isn't just a shy girl with her nose buried in a book all the time, like I thought…"

"Do you want to go over and say hello?" Melanie raised her eyebrows inquisitively. "I could get that autograph…

"No," I sighed. "I'm sure the last thing she wants is for her big sister to come crash her party—I think I'll just get my food to go."

"Okay." Melanie nodded. "This place is going to get rowdy soon anyway."

I had a few bites of the appetizer, drank half of my margarita, and asked the waiter for the check. I caught a few glances of Anna snuggled in a booth next to the guy she was apparently dating—and she definitely looked like she was in love with him. I wondered if all her new privileged friends had any idea that she spent her evenings reading books instead of trying to figure out how to spend her money—money she didn't even have. Even if I didn't like the privileged, I was happy for her. My high school years were hell because of people like them—and would have been a lot worse if Victoria hadn't stuck up for me a few times. High school love was unlikely to last forever, but at least Anna was having fun. She smiled so much she practically glowed.

I wonder if I have that same kind of glow when Bryant looks at me...

Chapter Twelve

BRYANT

The next day

*I*t was a normal Friday at Benson Enterprises—except that all of the people in the office were extremely excited that they were going to get lunch from Moretti's. Cassie spent the morning gathering everyone's orders while I met with some potential new clients. I was surprised to see that Danny Fontenot's name was on my list for the afternoon. I knew his financial situation had changed based on the conversation we had at Chateau Prime, but if he wanted to discuss investment opportunities, then he must have been doing better than I realized. Benson Enterprises catered to clients that had a *lot* of money to invest.

"Mr. Benson, do you have a moment?" One of my account managers, a woman named Kara James, knocked on my door shortly before lunch.

"Uh…" I looked at my calendar. "Yes, it looks like I'm free until after lunch."

"Thank you." She walked into my office and closed the door. "I hope I'm not out of line here…"

That's what people say right before they forget lines exist and step over them, so...

"Please, have a seat." I motioned to the chair in front of my desk.

"I just wanted to bring something to your attention." She walked over and sat down—I could tell she was nervous. "We've got some worried people in the office, and I thought it would be best if it was brought to your attention."

"Worried?" I blinked in surprise. "About Moretti's?"

"No sir. This isn't about lunch—we're really happy about that." She shook her head quickly and swallowed like she was suppressing a gulp. "The meeting—the one you had with Alexis Devereaux."

"It was nothing." I waved off her concern.

"I believe you, and I suspected as much. I've worked here too long to think that you would do business with someone like her—but people need to *hear* that." She looked down and sighed.

"You're right." I nodded. "Thank you for bringing this to my attention. I'll talk to everyone right after lunch."

"Thank you." She smiled and leaned forward to stand.

I appreciated Kara's visit. I always tried to keep an open-door policy at Benson Enterprises, just like my father did, and it existed because of situations like the one I was in. It was best to deal with the concerns immediately—my employees were too loyal to be kept in suspense or worry about trivial shit like Alexis's visit. I decided to at least let them enjoy lunch, but I knew that would also give Kara time to tell a few people what I said. That would set the atmosphere and ease some tensions before I made my speech.

"Here's your order, Mr. Benson." Cassie walked into my office with a smile on her face and placed my lunch special from Moretti's on my desk.

"Thanks." I nodded and pulled it over. "Fork?"

"Oh, right—be right back." Cassie disappeared through the door and returned with a set of plastic utensils. "Anything else?"

"Nah, I'm good. Let everyone know that I will be holding a quick meeting after lunch." I looked up at her and nodded.

"Yes sir." She turned back towards the door.

The lunch from Moretti's wasn't quite as good as dining in, but it was certainly better than most of the other options we could have gone with. I felt bad that I didn't cancel my reservations when Taylor and I decided to skip out on dinner, but I didn't feel bad about what we did with that time. I just had to make it through the rest of the day, and then the weekend would be ours. I had no intention of planning a date for us—I was just going to wait and see how the day went. There was a damn good chance we wouldn't even make it out of bed. I certainly wasn't going to complain if we didn't.

Okay, time to meet with the team, and then I only have a couple more meetings before I can call it a night.

"Can I have everyone's attention?" I walked out of my office and found most of the team already gathered in anticipation of the meeting.

"Kara, will you round up everyone that isn't here?" Cassie walked over and started assessing the attendance—making sure we didn't have any stragglers for our meetings was one of her jobs.

"Right way." Kara looked around the room and headed out to the floor where a few people were still finishing their lunch.

"Thank you for lunch, Mr. Benson." One of my newer employees, Paul, stepped forward and gave me a nod.

"Just a token of my appreciation—nothing more." I smiled and gave him a nod in response.

It took a few minutes for Kara to round up everyone that wasn't already gathered for our meeting. I filled the time with a few compliments for those that had been doing an exceptional job, another *thank you* to those that came in to work through the weekend when we had our emergency, and cracked a few jokes. The atmosphere didn't seem to be as tense as Kara described, but there was a good chance that they were just afraid to show their concern. I had tried to relax things a little bit since I took over. My father wasn't a difficult boss by any means, but the millennial generation expected a little more, and I tried to accommodate them.

"Okay I think that's everyone." I stepped forward and looked around the room. "Kara brought something to my attention, and I need to address it with everyone. I know some of you have concerns about my recent meeting with Alexis Devereaux…"

Yep, that sucked the energy out of the room really quick.

"First, let me assure you that her visit wasn't scheduled—and I would never do business with her." I made eye contact with a few people in the room. "I know a lot of you are here right now because her ex-husband took over the company you devoted your life to. That isn't going to happen to Benson Enterprises—you have my word."

I watched as people processed what I said. There were a few questions, and I answered them with ease. It seemed to be enough to quell the concerns and confirm that the job security they thought they enjoyed prior to seeing Alexis in my office would still provide the stability they needed to take care of their families. After I was sure everyone was okay with my explanation, I headed back to my office so that I could finish the rest of my work for the day. It was hard to focus on that with Taylor on my mind—I was looking forward to Saturday more than I had looked forward to a weekend in a very long time.

A couple of meetings and I can think about the weekend from the comfort of my own home.

The next day

I woke up so early that the sun wasn't even up yet—hell, it still had a couple of hours before it peeked through the clouds. I tried to force myself to go back to sleep, but I just couldn't get my mind to shut down. I finally gave up and went downstairs so I could fix some coffee and watch television. I caught the tail end of a movie that I hadn't seen in a while, so I finished it. The movie that came on after it was over kept me slightly entertained for a couple of hours, and then I went upstairs to shower and brush my teeth. I could feel the lack of sleep, even with caffeine in my veins, so I relaxed until I got a text message from Taylor—she was five minutes away.

I should have squeezed in a workout since I was up early—but then again, I think I'll be getting one that puts my time in the gym to shame before the day is over.

"Good morning!" I opened the door as soon as Taylor parked in the driveway and smiled as she approached.

"I hope I'm not too early…" She looked up at me with concern on her face as she ascended the steps.

"No, you're right on time." I pulled her into my arms and immediately went for a kiss.

Feeling Taylor's lips against mine was enough to purge the weariness I had from getting up early. My pulse started racing, and my heart began to beat in my ears. I pulled her into the house—and we made it to the couch before our passion really began to consume us. It wasn't long before our shirts were off, her bra was hanging on the arm of the couch, and my lips were exploring her body. We definitely needed to take it to the bedroom soon, but we had a lot of fun on the couch the first night we were together, so I wasn't in a hurry—we had all day.

"I missed you so much." I pulled her close and kissed my way up to her ear.

"I missed you too…" She moaned, and goosebumps began to spread across her skin.

"I'm going to do so many things to you today," I exhaled into her ear. "I'm going to kiss your ears—your neck—your breasts—and then I'm going to have a taste of what I've been craving since you left…"

"If you do that…" She moved her hand up my thigh and squeezed my cock through my pants. "I'm going to get down on my knees and make you come."

We continued whispering dirty things to each other as I unfastened Taylor's jeans and started to play with her pussy. It was already wet—and I wanted a taste so fucking bad. I shifted her jeans down her hips, and her panties slid with them. Our lips met for another kiss, which caused me to get temporarily distracted, but feeling her lips against mine was worth it. I finished removing her jeans, along with her panties, and stared at the sight of her beautiful curves before I started to devour them—every swirl of my tongue—every tease against her skin —brought me closer to the paradise that I craved. I teased her inner thighs, forced her legs apart, and heard her moan as my tongue got dangerously close to her clit—but then she put a hand on my shoulder and sat up suddenly.

"What was that?" She looked at me with concern on her face.

"Huh? What do you mean?" I raised an eyebrow.

"I heard something…" She reached down and grabbed her shirt. "It was a car door."

"Really?" I lifted off the couch and adjusted my clothes before walking to the window—my eyes nearly bulged out of my head. "Oh fuck! It's Dylan!"

"Where do I go?" Taylor's voice was panicked, and she started frantically gathering up her clothes.

"Uh—there!" I pointed to the bathroom. "I'll tell him there's a problem with it and send him to the west wing of the house if he needs to go."

Taylor picked up all of her clothes and dashed into the bathroom—the door slammed right before Dylan started walking towards the house. I had no idea why he was home—but judging by the duffel bag he was carrying, it looked like he was planning to stay with me for the weekend. It wasn't uncommon for him to come home, but he usually called first—hell, he normally let me know at least a week in advance in case I had something going on at work. I thought about meeting him at the door but decided to make it seem as nonchalant as possible. I grabbed my tablet, sat down in one of the chairs in the living room—and spotted Taylor's panties peeking out from under the couch. I barely had time to stuff them into my pocket before the front door opened and my son walked in.

"Dylan?" I tried to keep a calm expression and pretend to be totally surprised—like I didn't already know he was walking up to the door. "I didn't know you were coming home this weekend."

"Hey Dad." He walked into the living room and tossed his duffel bag on the couch. "Sorry I didn't call—it was kind of a last minute thing. One of my high school buddies wants to get the gang together—he's proposing to his girl and we're all friends, so he wanted us there."

"Ah." I stood up and put down my tablet so I could give him a hug. "Welcome home."

So far, so good…

"Is someone here?" He gave me a quick hug and pulled away. "There's a car in the driveway."

Fuck…

"Yeah…" I quickly tried to wrack my brain. "I hired a new

cleaning service—their car broke down. I think they're coming back to get it later."

"Oh, okay." He nodded. "I thought it might be someone I know. They have an old Carson Cove Tigers sticker in the back window."

"I don't know." I shrugged. "Maybe they have a kid in high school…"

Okay, it's turning into a string of lies, but it looks like he's buying it.

"I need to run to the restroom—long drive." He patted my shoulder and started walking towards the one that Taylor was hiding in.

"Wait." I grabbed his arm. "I'm having some trouble with that one and I haven't called a plumber yet."

"Alright, I'll run upstairs. Maybe I can take a look at it when I get back—I had to fix the one in my dorm last semester." He grabbed his duffel bag and walked towards the stairs.

I hated lying to my son, but I had no idea how I would explain Taylor's presence if he saw her—and he knew she was Victoria's best friend. As soon as Dylan was upstairs, I checked on Taylor in the bathroom. She was fully dressed, except for her panties that were still in my pocket. I couldn't usher her out the front door, and if the car disappeared while he was upstairs, it would probably look suspicious. We didn't get much time to figure it out, because I heard Dylan coming back downstairs.

"Hide in the library." I motioned down the hallway. "He never goes in there."

"Okay." Taylor nodded and made a dash for it—as quietly as possible.

The morning went from one that was supposed to be filled with excitement to a stressful endeavor. Dylan couldn't find anything wrong with the toilet—because there wasn't—and I pretended to be a dolt that made a mistake. As soon as he went upstairs to make a few calls and check in with his friends, I went to the library to see how Taylor was holding up. Needless to say, she wasn't happy. She just wanted to go—but I was worried she wouldn't make it out the front door in time.

I mildly hoped that would leave to meet his friends early, but that wasn't the case—he came back downstairs and told me they weren't meeting up until the afternoon. Normally, I would have welcomed any opportunity to see my son, but his timing was horrible. If I had known he was coming, I would have never planned to spend Saturday with Taylor—and I didn't know if she was going to forgive me for holding her prisoner all day if it came to that.

"Hey Dad?" Dylan walked back into the living room and sat down across from me—in the same spot where I was undressing Taylor shortly before he arrived.

"Yeah?" I looked up at him.

"Something I wanted to ask you…" He looked down and sighed. "Have you talked to Victoria or Shaina lately?"

"Yeah." I shrugged. "You don't keep in touch with your sisters? That's surprising…"

"I do—well, I have been." He had a slightly worried expression on his face, which caused me to tense up. "I haven't been able to get in touch with Shaina for a couple of weeks. Victoria said she hadn't heard from her either…"

"I talked to Shaina…" I looked up and tried to remember the last conversation. "Well damn, yeah—I talked to her a couple of weeks ago, but I didn't get a call back from her when I tried to call last weekend."

I've been so preoccupied with everything else—but I just assumed she was busy with law school.

"I wasn't really that close to Shaina growing up, but we still try to keep in touch, you know?" he sighed. "She's probably got stuff going on—law school and all."

"Yeah." I nodded, but the worry didn't leave me

completely—I definitely needed to try to call her again. "I'm sure she's okay."

Dylan has more important things to worry about. I'll figure out what is going on with Shaina.

"How are things going with you?" I leaned forward. "Grades still holding up?"

"Of course," he smirked. "I'm not a slouch like Victoria."

"She's doing fine," I chuckled under my breath. "Good enough to graduate—that's all that really matters."

"I want to graduate at the top of my class." He shrugged, and the smirk didn't leave his face. "I have to be able to get a good job when I'm done with college—can't leech off you forever, old man."

"I wish I could convince you to come work for me at Benson Enterprises. My chair will be yours one day." I raised an eyebrow.

"Yeah, I know." He nodded. "I just want to get some experience and see what else is out there—I might have some new ideas when I finally do some work for you."

Maybe he'll change his mind before graduation—he's still got a few years to do that.

I knew part of the reason Dylan didn't want to move back to Carson Cove and start working at Benson Enterprises right after graduation was because he missed his mother. He didn't say that, but they were always close—he was our youngest, so he got to be the baby longer than Shaina or Victoria did. It was no coincidence that he was thinking about working in the city after graduation, which was where she moved after the divorce. He didn't get to see her very often. It was easy enough to make a trip to Carson Cove for the weekend, but it was a long drive to the city.

"Oh, speaking of people that you haven't talked to in a while…" Dylan seemed to hesitate, and he looked down before he continued speaking. "Mom is working now. She got a job at Dillinger Tech."

I didn't think he'd actually bring her up—he must think the wound has finally started to scar. It has, but he has no idea why...

"Really?" I raised my eyebrows in surprise. "Did my last alimony check bounce or something?"

That was a little harsher than I intended, but it's hard to hold back— she was the one who decided to file for divorce.

"I think she's just bored." He leaned back against the couch.

My comment seemed to sour Dylan's mood a little bit and normally I would have apologized, but I was distracted by other things—namely Taylor, who was still hiding in the library. Dylan and I continued discussing his future, how things were going at school, and he let it slip that he had a girlfriend—which I decided to start calling *mystery girl* as a tease since he wouldn't tell me her name. I finally found a break in the conversation and excused myself. I blamed it on work, which would explain why I was going to the library. Taylor had been in there for almost two hours, and if she wasn't angry, it would be a blessing.

"Hey…" I pushed the door open and found her sitting at my desk reading a book.

"Is he gone?" She put the book down and stood.

"No, I'm so fucking sorry." I walked over and hugged her. "I'll get you out of here as soon as I can."

"I never thought I would be hiding in here from your son— usually I was hiding from *you* when I was exploring this place." She leaned back from our embrace and grinned.

"We already addressed *that* behavior," I chuckled under my breath and kissed her forehead.

"Some of it…" She bit down on her lip and giggled.

I'd love to have a long discussion about it upstairs, but that isn't possible now.

"Damn it—I was looking forward to spending the day with you." I exhaled sharply and shook my head.

"It'll be okay. I'll find a way to entertain myself..." She shrugged and sat back down.

I couldn't do much more than apologize—and I couldn't stay in the library long or I would risk Dylan coming to check on me. A part of me just wanted to rip the mask off the charade and tell him the truth, but it wouldn't be fair to Taylor —she was still Victoria's best friend, and there was no way Dylan would keep our secret. He was too close to his sister for me to ask him to choose sides—*and* choose mine. If my relationship with Taylor continued, we would have to tell Victoria the truth, but that conversation was best had in person.

"Everything okay at Benson Enterprises?" Dylan looked up at me when I returned.

"Yeah, just had to check in on a few things." I nodded and sat down.

Dylan and I hung out for a little bit longer, ate lunch, and I managed to sneak a plate to Taylor after he returned to the living room. It was another hour before he decided to shower and get ready to meet his friends. As soon as he was upstairs, I hurried Taylor to the front door and gave her a quick kiss before she took off. I considered asking her to come back after Dylan was gone, but I had no idea how long he would be out with his friends. He wasn't much of a partier, so he didn't normally stay out late when he was visiting Carson Cove. Taylor didn't seem angry with me at all, but I could see a hint of disappointment in her eyes before she walked to the car. I watched until she was gone and let out a sigh of relief since the crisis had been averted.

I'll make it up to you, Taylor—I just don't know how yet.

Chapter Thirteen

TAYLOR

I kept my composure with Bryant, but I was in full-blown panic mode when I left Benson Estate. In the back of mind, I knew there was always a risk—if we didn't get caught in the act, someone who knew Victoria could see us when we were together. I was convinced that she would believe my intentions were pure if she had found out after the art show —but the purity didn't last long. If someone told her about the kiss—it would be *really* hard to explain. If Dylan had realized I was at Benson Estate when he arrived, then there would have been *no* explanation that made sense. I had hours to let the guilt toy with me, and it was beginning to become unbearable. I was falling for Bryant, but the reality of the situation made a relationship impossible—the sooner I accepted that, the better it would be for both of us.

The longer it drags on, the more it's going to hurt when the inevitable tears us apart.

"You're home?" Anna poked her head out of her room when I walked upstairs. "I thought you were planning to stay out late."

"My plans changed." I shrugged. "It looks like I'm spending Saturday night at home—maybe we can hang out?"

"Uh…" She looked down. "I have plans."

"Is that so?" I couldn't help but smile. "Do you want to talk about those plans?"

"No." She shook her head back and forth.

"Just be careful, Anna—please." I wanted to say more, but I didn't want her to know that I saw her with Bolt—especially if she wasn't ready to talk about it.

"I'm always careful." She rolled her eyes. "Mom won't be home either—she got called into work, and she's going out with some of the girls from the office tonight."

"Great…" I sighed. "I guess it's Netflix for me."

"You could always paint me something…" She raised an eyebrow.

"So you can tell me that you hate it?" I looked down and laughed. "Nah, I don't think I'm in the mood."

I walked into my room and changed into my pajamas. If I was spending Saturday night at home, I preferred to be comfortable. There was also no reason for me to watch a movie in my room if nobody was home—the television downstairs was much bigger and had surround sound. I found a movie that sounded interesting but decided to play on my phone for a little while before I started it. I couldn't help but notice that Anna was actually wearing makeup and some jeans that were rather tight when she finally did come downstairs. I pretended not to notice. I still hadn't gotten used to the idea of my little sister hanging out with the privileged, and if Bolt was a star football player at Carson Cove High, he was an honorary one, even if he didn't have the bank account to back it up.

Maybe she'll have more fun in high school than I did—not that I had any interest in mingling with the privileged back then.

After Anna left, I made a frozen pizza and fixed a glass of

wine—it wasn't the best combination in the world, but it was what we had in the house. My mother usually bought groceries on Sunday, so it was pretty barren by the weekend. I carried my dinner into the living room and started my movie. It was slow in the beginning, and the wine put me in a different mood, so I didn't make it very far—I decided to find something with more humor than drama. My second movie was kind of raunchy, but rather funny, and I found myself laughing at jokes that would have normally gotten little more than a roll of my eyes. I was about midway through the movie and considering a third glass of wine when my phone lit up—I had a message from Bryant.

Bryant: Have you forgiven me yet?

Taylor: I told you I wasn't mad…

Bryant: I know but I still feel bad about it.

Taylor: Is Dylan still there?

Bryant: No, he went out with friends. I don't know when he'll be back. I wish you were here…

Taylor: Maybe next weekend.

Bryant: You're really going to make me wait an entire week?

Taylor: When does Dylan leave?

Bryant: If it's like most of his visits, he'll stay until Monday, and get up early so he can drive back to school before his first class.

Taylor: Then I guess you have to wait. :(

Bryant: You can't sneak in a visit during the week?

Taylor: I'll have to see how things go with school.

Bryant: Okay.

I might have been convinced to squeeze in a visit to Bryant on Sunday night if Dylan was leaving—even though I was still wracked with a fair amount of guilt over almost being caught. I was dancing on a razor blade, and one false step would cut me in two but didn't know how to shut off the part of me that was falling for him. We kept texting back and forth—I had another glass of wine, but left my movie paused because talking to him was a lot more interesting than the comedy on the screen in front of me.

Bryant: Send me a picture...

Taylor: No way, I'm already in my pajamas and my hair is a mess.

Bryant: So? You can take your pajamas off it makes you feel better...

Taylor: You'd like that, wouldn't you?

Bryant: Very much... Come on. I may have to wait an entire week to see you!

Taylor: Fine...

I took the best picture I could, but I wasn't very happy with it, so I snapped a few more to try and get a better shot. None of them were perfect, but I finally found one that I considered acceptable to send. I still ran it through a few filters to adjust the color, hide some of the background, and smooth over a few of the blemishes I hated. I always criticized the people who didn't post anything on Facebook unless it had been heavily filtered, but there I was—doing the exact same thing, like some kind of hypocrite. I hit the button and sent it to Bryant once it was as perfect as it was ever going to be.

Taylor: Here you go...

Bryant: Wow, beautiful!

Taylor: Do I get one of you?

Bryant: I guess that's fair.

It didn't take long for Bryant to send a response, and he didn't use a single filter—he didn't need them. It was a casual picture of him on the couch with the top few buttons of his shirt unbuttoned. It should have been a crime to look that hot without trying—just seeing a picture of him was enough to make my body tingle. There was something about Bryant that made me temporarily lose my connection with rational thought —I knew it was forbidden, dangerous, and even exchanging text messages with him was a risk if one of his kids looked at his phone. Every time I convinced myself I was going to pull away before it was too late, I found myself thinking about having his lips against mine—feeling them on my skin—and being in his arms.

Taylor: I wish I was there with you right now.

Bryant: I would do so many things to you if you were...

Taylor: Dirty things? :)

Bryant: You know the answer already. I would finish what we started earlier today.

The conversation started to get quite flirty—with a hint of dirty—and Bryant asked for another picture. I decided to send him one that was a little more risqué than the first one I sent. I unbuttoned my pajama top, leaned forward, and took one that showed my breasts without revealing my nipples. That got me one of him without a shirt, and I'm surprised my cell phone didn't melt in my hand—it was so hot that my hand trembled, and my mouth fell open. I really wanted to be there with him —I wanted to feel the same pleasure he showed me when he took my innocence. He made me feel carefree—despite the danger—and for the first time in my life, I felt *sexy*. I snapped a few more pictures, sent them to him, and was tempted to take one that showed more skin—but my phone lit up while I was trying to figure out the angle. It wasn't a message from Bryant —it was from Victoria.

Oh god...

Victoria: Hey girl! Long time! How are you doing?

Panic immediately swept through me—there was no way for her to know I was literally exchanging dirty messages and pictures with her father—or had some strange daughterly intuition made her message me out of the blue? I quickly fired off a message to Bryant to let him know that I had something come up. He was disappointed that I was bringing the conversation to an abrupt end, but I couldn't sit there and continue it while I exchanged messages with Victoria. Just staring at her message made me sick to my stomach—it brought every *bad* thing we were doing back into perspective immediately and left me with a sense of dread. I had no choice but to reply—even if it made me want to just crawl in a hole instead.

Taylor: Hey! I'm good... I'm spending Saturday night on the couch watching Netflix, how about you?

Victoria: Girl, same! I was behind on a few assignments, so I spent the day working. Now it's time to relax...

Victoria sent me a picture of herself holding a glass of wine and angled it so I could see that she had a movie going in the background. That meant she wanted a message from me—and my wine glass was empty. I quickly ran to the kitchen, refilled it, and put my pajamas back on before starting my movie back up. I took a similar picture and sent it to her, once I applied a few filters to hide the fact that my makeup was long gone—not that Victoria cared, but she had surprised me once by posting a picture I sent her on social media. Once again—I was being a hypocrite—in more ways than one considering the fact that I was literally sending pictures to her father before she messaged me.

Victoria: I watched that movie! It was good!

Taylor: Yeah, it's really funny!

Victoria: How are things going in Carson Cove?

Taylor: Same as always, I guess.

Victoria: Have you heard any rumors? :)

Taylor: What kind of rumors?

Victoria: About my dad...

Oh god. She knows something. Fuck!

Taylor: I don't think so... We don't exactly run in the same circles. Why?

"Should I tell her the truth? This is my opportunity... I could tell her about the art show—I don't have to tell her everything." I started muttering to myself.

Victoria: One of my sister's friends messaged me—she was trying to get in touch with her and asked if I knew where she was. She also mentioned that my dad was seen with some mystery woman...

"If she knew it was me, she would just say something... Now I'm talking to myself like a crazy person," I sighed and took a sip of my wine. "I need to be as honest as possible here —it will ruin our friendship if I don't—I just can't tell her everything."

Taylor: I won tickets to the art show the other day, and he was there... I saw him talking to Alexis Devereaux...

I wanted to keep typing—and reveal as much of the truth as possible without telling her that I had spent one unforgettable night in her father's bed. My fingers hesitated before I could say what happened after I saw Alexis talking to her father. I typed another sentence—erased it—typed another one —then erased it too.

Victoria: He would never date someone like her. She's a pariah.

Taylor: Yeah, I don't think she got anywhere.

Victoria: What a fucking bitch. Maybe that's what they saw...

Taylor: Maybe...

Victoria: Hopefully, he's not involved with anyone. Especially her.

Taylor: It took me a while to get used to the idea of my parents dating too...

Victoria: I would have been fine with it under normal circumstances...

Taylor: What do you mean?

Victoria: My mom isn't doing well. She thought she knew what she wanted with the divorce... Damn it; she told me not to tell anyone. I know you won't say anything though.

Taylor: No, of course not...

Victoria: She's all alone in the city, and she's having a lot of regrets right now. My brother visits when he can, but she doesn't feel like she can really talk to him—he's still her baby.

Taylor: The price of being the youngest...

Victoria: Yeah. My mom just misses her family right now—and I think she misses my dad too, even though she won't admit it. I've been trying to convince her to reach out to him. I don't know if a reconciliation is possible... She hurt him.

Taylor: I'm sure it would be difficult...

Victoria: I know. I might make a trip home to talk to him—or at least talk to her in person.

My guilt immediately went through the roof—the panic that had been twisting my stomach into a knot made me begin to hyperventilate. My head spun, and I felt like I couldn't get enough oxygen. More wine was probably the last thing I needed, but I downed the entire glass and ran to the kitchen for more. It didn't make me feel any better, but it was wet— and after a few more sips, my breathing returned to normal. Victoria would be upset if she came home and found out that I was involved with her father—there was a good chance it would end our friendship—but if she thought I was standing between her parents and reconciliation, then she would abso- lutely *hate* me.

I have to end things with Bryant. I have to stop saying that I will— and actually do it—no matter how good he makes me feel.

I exchanged a few more text messages with Victoria and tried to steer clear of the subject I didn't want to discuss. I asked about school, guys she was dating—basically anything that would ensure she didn't start talking about her parents again. It had been a while since we talked but I was absolutely relieved when the conversation finally began to wind down. I had way too much wine and was ready for the bed. I certainly didn't want Anna or my mom to walk in and find me in the living room drunk. The movie I was watching ended at some point, but I had no idea what happened towards the end—it didn't matter. It wasn't going to make me laugh anymore— nothing could do that.

I need to see Bryant as soon as possible. I don't want to risk this drag- ging out until next weekend—I don't know if Victoria will come home immediately or wait until things settle down at school.

The next day

I don't know how I managed to actually fall asleep—it was probably all of the wine in my system that put me down for the count. I tossed and turned for a little while and actually heard Anna arrive shortly before my mom did. Even though I *did* fall asleep, I didn't sleep well. My dreams were chaotic and filled with flashing scenes of my worst fears— getting caught with Bryant—the look on Victoria's face when she found out we were together—and the one that woke me up was of him getting remarried to his ex-wife. That's what it appeared to be at least—until he raised her veil, and I saw Alexis Devereaux underneath it. It was a dream so horrifying that I woke up in a cold sweat with the sun peeking through the clouds.

I'm definitely not going back to sleep after that.

When I was younger, I had a lot of reasons for painting— and one of them was because it helped me process my emotions with a certain level of clarity. My easel was turned around and the last painting I was working on was facing the closet—it was supposed to be a landscape, but I wasn't in the mood for that. I replaced it with a fresh canvas, mixed up some paint, and let my emotions flow through the end of the paint- brush. Three hours later, I had a painting that was filled with dark imagery, and a splotchy outline of a woman crying orange tears. I had no idea why they were orange—and the woman didn't resemble anyone I knew—but it seemed to capture the turmoil that was tearing my soul in half.

I wish it was possible to cry it all away—that would be easier than facing the truth.

I heard my sister's bedroom door open, and a few minutes later, my mother's did as well. I decided to join them—except my pajamas had a few smears of paint, so I quickly changed into a fresh set of clothes. The painting I created was personal, and even though my mother had lost her love of art, she would have still asked to see it if she knew I was working on something new. Anna probably would too—just because it had been a while since I picked up a brush. It was too emotional to share, and I wouldn't be able to tell them where the inspiration came from. It was just too damn complicated to explain.

It's a good thing it isn't socially acceptable to have wine for breakfast…

Chapter Fourteen

BRYANT

The next day

*D*ylan stayed all weekend, and I tried to let myself get absorbed with work when he wasn't around. If I didn't have something to distract me, the only thing on my mind was Taylor. I wanted to find a way show her that I was sorry our date didn't work out, and I hated that I was going to have to wait an entire week to do it. I wasn't upset with Dylan for visiting—I loved spending time with my son—it was just poor timing because I didn't know he was coming until he showed up at my door.

I tried to call Shaina a couple of times on Sunday, but I wasn't able to reach her. I did talk to Victoria for a little while, and she said she hadn't been able to get in touch with her either. By the time I made it to work on Monday morning, I was starting to worry more about my oldest daughter than when I would see Taylor again. It wasn't unusual for Shaina to get busy with school and miss a few calls, but she normally called me back—at some point. The silence didn't sit well with me, especially since Dylan and Victoria hadn't been able to get in touch with her either—that definitely wasn't normal.

"Cassie, I need you to do something for me." I walked out of my office after my first morning meeting.

"Yes sir, what do you need?" She looked up at me.

"I need you to place a call to Shaina's school—if they need to talk to me, it's fine, but I want to know if she made it to class today." I looked around the office and sighed. "I haven't been able to get in touch with her."

"I'll take care of it." She nodded and started searching for the number.

I went back to my office, looked over a few reports, and made some decisions regarding our investments for the week. Cassie had to leave a message, so it turned into a waiting game. The worry intensified as the day wore on, and by the afternoon, I was starting to lose my mind. Cassie could tell that it was really bothering me, so she called back—and refused to let them just take another message. She stayed on hold for nearly ten minutes, but someone with a little bit of authority finally came on the line. It shouldn't have taken that long considering that I made donations to Shaina's school, on top of paying her tuition. I was just about to walk over and take over the conversation when my cell phone lit up, and I saw Shaina's number.

"She's calling me." I waved Cassie off and headed to my office. "Hello?"

"Hey Dad!" It was Shaina's voice—and she sounded rather cheerful.

"Shaina..." I sat down behind my desk. "Why haven't you returned my calls—Dylan and Victoria said they were having trouble getting in touch with you too..."

"Oh, I'm sorry. I've just been really busy with school—I spent the whole weekend in the library researching a case that I have to present..." she exhaled into the receiver.

"Last week too?" I narrowed my eyes.

"It's just been…" she sighed. "Really busy."

"Okay." I decided to drop it—I was talking to her—she sounded fine. "Please make sure you stay in touch. You know we're going to worry if you don't…"

"I know." Her voice trailed off for a second. "I love you, Dad."

"I love you too…" I closed my eyes and tried to calm down —the worry hadn't left me completely. "How is everything going—outside of the case you're working on."

"Everything is fine…" A muffled sound echoed, and it sounded like she put her hand over the phone. "Hey, I gotta go. I just wanted to make sure you knew I was okay."

"Sure, no problem. Maybe we can talk later this week?" I leaned back in my chair.

"Definitely! I'll call you." There was another muffled sound, and then she hung up.

I quickly sent a message to Dylan and Victoria so they would know that I heard from Shaina. Cassie came into my office and told me that she confirmed Shaina had been attending classes regularly. The crisis was seemingly averted— everything was fine. I just had to keep reminding myself that my kids were grown, and they were living their own lives. There was a good chance that we would grow further apart once they graduated—a weekly call would become a luxury instead of an expectation. My ex-wife and I always joked that we were going to have another baby after the three we already had were in high school—just to avoid empty nest syndrome. There was no chance of that happening anymore, and I wasn't sure I would be up for it, even if there was a way for it to happen.

That may become a point of contention with Taylor—but our relationship isn't far enough along to think about it now.

I got back on track with my meetings for the afternoon once I confirmed Shaina was safe. The other people in the office left, including Cassie, but I stayed behind to catch up on some work. It wasn't like I had anyone waiting at home—and I wasn't going to be able to see Taylor until the weekend if she couldn't find time to sneak away from her schoolwork. I hated it—especially after getting interrupted over the weekend, but we would just have to make up for lost time when we were together. Taylor must have sensed that I was thinking about her, because my phone lit up and I saw her number on the screen.

Taylor: Hey…

Bryant: Hello beautiful.

Taylor: I don't have as many assignments as I expected. Can I come over?

Bryant: Give me time to get home. :)

Taylor: Okay. There's something we need to talk about…

Bryant: Oh? Is there a problem?

Taylor: Let's just discuss it in person.

Bryant: I should be home in about an hour.

It seemed that I had traded one worry for another—I didn't have to worry about Shaina anymore, but Taylor's message was ominous. Experience had taught me that it usually wasn't a good sign when a woman said they needed to talk—but I had no idea what could have happened. We talked over the weekend—we traded a few dirty pictures—everything seemed to be fine. If the roles were reversed, I'm not sure I would have been as calm as she was when Dylan interrupted us —I certainly wouldn't have been happy about being locked in a library all day like someone was ashamed of me. That wasn't the reason—the reason we needed to keep things secret meant just as much to her as it did to me—possibly more. All I could do was drive to my house and wait—that didn't do anything to ease the tension, especially when I heard her car pull up in the driveway.

"Hey…" I opened the door as she walked up the steps.

I decided not to wait and just let things unfold without having a say in it—the look on her face told me that she wasn't happy. I immediately pulled her into my arms and kissed her before a word could leave those perfectly pouty lips. I felt hesitation for a moment, but then she melted into my embrace, and her kiss was as fierce as mine. Our lips stayed seared together as she crossed the threshold into my house, and I kicked the door closed because I didn't want to take my hands off her. The kiss brought all of the passion to the surface, and I started kissing my way down her neck and up to her ear as soon as we were forced to gasp for air.

"What did you want to tell me?" I teased her ear with my lips as I whispered into it.

"I…" One single word; followed by a sigh.

"You want to pick up where we left off on Saturday?" I kissed her neck and squeezed her ass. "Was that it?"

"Yes…" She nodded and moaned when I moved my hands to the front of her jeans.

I didn't think that was really what she intended to say—but I wasn't going to press for more, because I was scared it would pull her out of my arms. If she was doubting what we had, or letting her thoughts get in the way of something, then I needed to show her how much I had craved her touch—her lips—and her gorgeous curves. I pulled at her clothes as we made our way to the living room—slowly—with the passion getting stronger by the second. We left a trail of clothes on the way to the couch and she wasn't wearing anything but her panties when she fell against the cushions—and I was on top of her in an instant.

"I didn't get a taste of you—not like I wanted." I exhaled sharply into her ear. "I'm going to pick up *right* where I left off."

"Wait…" She moaned and squirmed underneath me. "I—I can't stay that long."

"It won't take long." I slid my hand into her panties and started rubbing her pussy. "You're already so fucking wet…"

"Just—make love to me…" she moaned.

There was something left unsaid—a *but* that lingered on her lips but never passed across them. Her eyes betrayed her. I wanted her more than I wanted anything else in the world in that moment, but something was truly bothering her. I started to lift up—it was better to say what needed to be said rather than let it linger—but Taylor no longer wanted to talk. She grabbed the front of my shirt and pulled me back down—her lips found mine, and I just let the concern fade away. Her kiss was filled with too much passion for the problem to be that serious—it could have been a million things, but only one of them mattered—she wanted me as much as I wanted her. I wrapped my fingers around her panties, stripped them off her hips, and she started furiously pulling at my clothes.

Whatever needs to be said can wait—obviously it's not as important as the desire burning inside both of us.

"Those pictures were nice…" I squeezed her breasts, moved my hands down to her hips, and forced her legs apart. "But this is so much better."

My shirt hit the floor, and I kicked off my pants as soon as she got them pushed past my hips. I grabbed the base of my cock, brought it to her wetness, and gently pushed my way inside her. Her pussy fit me like a glove—it was so fucking tight, but her body adjusted to me a lot faster than it did the last time we were together. A couple of gentle thrusts made her moan—a few more of those made her gasp—and then I was able to go deeper.

I silenced her next gasp with a kiss and started to thrust harder—it didn't take many of those to bring our bodies together. She moaned against my lips as I began to ravage her mouth with my tongue, and my hips picked up speed. I finally `ad to pull away just to gasp for air, but my thrusts didn't slow down. Her breathing got heavier, and she started to move her hips in unison with mine.

"You feel so fucking good—I missed you so much," I leaned forward and growled into her ear. "You're mine—nothing can change that."

No words. No problems. Absolutely nothing. Whatever is bothering you—we can overcome it—just believe in what we have for one more night.

"Oh god..." She moaned louder, and her body began to shake. "You're gonna make me come."

"We may not have long—but I bet I can make you come a *lot* more than once." I drove my dick as deep as possible and then started to hammer her pussy.

I knew every complication that could be bothering her—the ones that made sense at least. They were lingering in my thoughts too, and I wasn't sure how we were going to get past them, but I was determined to find a way. She had done something to me—made me feel things that were practically forgotten before she walked into my life. Having her in my arms again confirmed what I already knew—letting her go was going to be impossible.

"Come for me," I exhaled sharply into her ear. "You know you want to."

"Yes!" She threw her head back and moaned.

Taylor's pussy started to spasm, and I didn't stop thrusting, even when the pleasure made my head spin. I wasn't ready to let go—not yet. I wanted to see the bliss on her face and hear those sweet moans as she realized I could make her come as many times as I wanted. As soon as the first orgasm began to fade, and she was no longer shaking, I brought her to the edge of another one. It still wasn't enough for me. The way she made me feel when she gave in was amazing—I wished I could get lost in that moment of euphoria forever. Nothing else mattered when we were together—all of those complications melted away as while we claimed the passion that existed solely for the two of us.

"Please…" Taylor dug her nails into my shoulders. "I want to feel you come."

"Give me one more," I growled into her ear. "Then you'll get what you want."

I was already struggling to hold back. I didn't have the benefit of a release before I was inside her like the first time we were together. I wanted to see the bliss one more time before I erupted—even if I wanted to give in so bad my balls were starting to ache. I thrust my cock into her pussy and made sure I was hitting her g-spot every time I went deep. Her body began to shake, and I knew she was close—her head rolled back, and her mouth opened wide. I silenced her scream with a kiss before it could leave her lips and felt the orgasm rip through her. That was all I could handle—I couldn't hold back any longer.

"Oh fuck…" I pulled my lips away from hers and a primal roar echoed in my throat.

Taylor's sweet orgasm made her pussy turn into my personal paradise as I began to come. A few quick thrusts made the cum surge through my shaft, and I unloaded my seed inside her. That was enough to make her taste bliss one more time, and the spasms milked me dry—I throbbed and pulsated until there was nothing left. My eruption sapped my strength and made my arms tremble. I pulled her close as I fell forward against the couch, and she was in my arms as I landed. Our lips met immediately, and a few tender kisses were shared as we let the afterglow of our passion take hold of us.

"I don't want to wait until the weekend to see you again…" I stroked her hair and stared into those pale emerald eyes.

"I just—I don't know…" She looked away.

"What did you want to talk to me about?" I tilted my head

slightly. "It sounded serious—I just wanted you so bad I couldn't hold back…"

I hope I erased whatever doubts she had—surely, she feels the connection that is forming between us.

"It was nothing." She looked up at the ceiling. "I was just having an emotional moment."

"Are you sure?" I tilted her chin until our eyes met again.

"Just hold me." She refused to hold eye contact and snuggled into my arms with her head against my chest.

"Okay…" I nodded and sighed.

Something is still bothering her, but she doesn't want to tell me what it is…

Taylor and I stayed tangled in our embrace for a couple of hours before she had to leave. I really didn't want her to go—especially if something was left unsaid—but she wasn't ready to talk about it. The passion we shared was intense, and I hoped that the lingering concerns she had faded while she was in my arms. I had no way to confirm it, but some of the dismay seemed to have faded from her eyes when she left. I wished I could read her thoughts—or maybe I didn't have to—maybe I was just seeing what I wanted to see when the harsh realities were right in front of my face. I didn't want to admit them to myself, because that was a road we couldn't come back from—it was laced with treachery and danger.

If this is going to work, we can't dance around the inevitable forever. Victoria may not understand, but I can't deny my feelings—and I don't want to hide what we have or lie about it.

The next day

I woke up in bed alone like I had every single day since my divorce. I hated it at first, but I got used to it as time confirmed our marriage was truly over. I didn't want my bed to be empty anymore when the sun peeked over the clouds. I wanted to see Taylor's gorgeous curves beside me— say *good morning* with a kiss—and find a way to get past the complications that she was hesitant to discuss. I didn't know how we were going to do that, but there had to be an answer to the question we were both hiding from.

It's not fair to have a heart beating in my chest if I can't share it with someone else—and I've finally found someone that could very well claim it if we can both find a way to give in.

I spent my morning tending to a few investments, reviewing several accounts that needed my attention, and meeting with my clients. I stared at my calendar after lunch and noticed Cassie had added an appointment in the afternoon that wasn't there when I started my day. It was with Jon—and I knew it wasn't going to be an easy one. My team had been working on his account for two days, and there was no way to easily fix his problem. He could save his company and still give his wife a good settlement in the divorce, but it would shred his finances to pieces. It would require him to start over, and it was a terrible option. Selling the company was the smartest move, but I knew he wouldn't be happy to hear that. Nothing about the situation was fair, and I was going to have to give him the bad news when he arrived.

"Mr. Benson." Cassie pushed my door open. "Mr. Alcott is here."

He's early—apparently, he doesn't want to wait to find out how bad it really is…

"Send him in." I stood up from my desk and walked over to pour a drink—he was going to need it.

"Yes sir." Cassie nodded and closed the door.

Fuck, there has to be a better way...

"I'm sorry I showed up early." Jon pushed my door open less than a minute after Cassie closed it.

"No problem." I handed him the drink as soon as he walked in. "Let's talk."

"What is there to talk about?" He sat down with a thud. "I already know I'm fucked..."

"I'm sorry, Jon." I sat down behind my desk and sighed.

"I got the notice this morning—the only way to keep my company is to go to trial and try to get a judge to enforce the original agreement." He took a gulp of his drink. "My lawyer says the chances of that happening are pretty fucking low."

"You still have to fight." I narrowed my eyes. "You can't give up."

"It's a fight that I won't win, no matter what." He took another drink. "The people I do business with? The blood will be in the water the instant they realize I may have to sell the company—distribution is a volatile business and if they think their sources might get compromised, they'll find someone else to handle their account."

"I'm sure your customers will be loyal..." I shook my head back and forth.

"If things are certain? Sure." He nodded. "But they don't know what will happen if someone buys the company. Hell, I don't even know myself. The new owner could raise prices, negotiate contracts with their competitors—all of the stuff I would never do."

"Fuck it." I leaned forward. "I'll buy Alcott Inc. Tell your lawyer to draw up the agreement."

"What?" Jon blinked in surprise.

I can't watch my best friend wallow in his own grief—nor can I stomach the thought of him losing everything.

"You'll stay on as CEO. Nothing will change. You can settle

with your ex-wife, and then you can buy the company back from me with the profits you make." I nodded quickly.

"Fuck man, I can't ask you to do that." He drained his glass and shook his head. "You have too much going on with Benson Enterprises."

"I trust you, Jon. I won't be involved with the company at all. It's basically a loan." I stood up and walked over to grab the whiskey so I could refill his glass.

Jon was practically brought to tears when he realized that I was serious. A handshake didn't make it official, but it did for me. Jon promised to have his lawyer get the paperwork together and clear the sale with his wife's new counsel. I doubted there would be any issues—she just wanted the money and didn't care where it came from.

I didn't have any meetings scheduled after Jon, so I was alone in my office once he was gone. I sent a couple of messages to Taylor to see if she would be able to see me, but she had too much going on with school. If I couldn't see her, the best thing to do was get some work done—especially since I was planning to buy Alcott Inc. I crunched a few numbers and realized that the purchase was going to stretch me thin. It wasn't enough to hurt, but I wouldn't be buying a Yacht anytime soon—not that I really had any intention of doing that anyway.

Jon doesn't deserve to lose everything he's worked for. Maybe this will take some sting out of the divorce and help him find a way to start healing —it's the least I can do.

Chapter Fifteen

TAYLOR

The next day

I should have ended things with Bryant. I went to his house with every intention of doing it, but I couldn't make myself say the words that needed to be said. I got lost in his stare—consumed by his touch—and as soon as he kissed me, the only place I wanted to be was in his arms. The *last* thing I should have done was melt into his embrace and have sex with him—that wasn't fair when I knew the relationship had to end.

Focusing on school with everything else tumbling around in my head was difficult. My first couple of classes just turned into a blur. Thankfully, the information my professors were relaying came straight out of my textbooks, so I could look over it at home when I had a little more clarity—not that I thought there was going to be a switch I could flip and get it. The only way I was going to be able to find peace was to do what was so damn difficult—and I couldn't keep delaying it if Victoria was planning to come home—especially if she wanted her parents to put aside their difference and reconcile. I had no idea if Bryant would go for it, but I didn't want to be the reason that he wasn't willing to consider it.

"You look like you're a million miles away." Melanie walked up to me in the hallway and gave me a nudge.

"Oh? Yeah…" I turned towards her. "I was just thinking about school stuff."

"Maybe my grades would be better if I stood in the hallway and daydreamed about my classes." She shook her head and laughed.

What the hell? Is that…why is she at my school?

"Uh…" I took a step to the side and motioned to the woman that was talking to one of the professors at Carson Cove University. "Why is Alexis Devereaux here?"

"Oh, her?" Melanie looked over her shoulder and shrugged. "She was invited by the dean to give a speech to some of the first-year students about being a successful woman in business—I guess you could call it a pep talk or something."

"What does she know about being a successful woman in business?" My words left my lips before I even thought about it.

Unless she opened her speech by telling them to marry a guy with a lot of money—and a successful company.

"You'd be surprised." Melanie turned back towards me. "There was a girl in one of my marketing classes who was upset that they didn't let seniors attend the speech. She said her dad used to work for Devereaux Properties and Alexis was the one calling the shots—she called her an inspiration."

"Weird…" I shifted again when Alexis looked down the hallway, just to make sure she didn't spot me.

"I guess people don't talk about it much, but she said Alexis' brother is a gambler and an alcoholic—the company would have gone under years ago if it wasn't for her." Melanie shrugged again. "Why do you care anyway?"

"Just curious…" I leaned against the wall. "I grew up in

Carson Cove—I've never heard of anyone clamoring for advice from the Devereaux family—not about business anyway."

I didn't have time to ponder it in the hallway—I needed to get to class. Thankfully, I was going in the opposite direction of Alexis. I knew the history of the Devereaux family—they were usually the talk of Carson Cove. I never had a face for their matriarch until I saw her at the art show. Her marriages usually started or ended with a scandal. Bryant had told me some things about her—and her last husband. I couldn't believe Carson Cove University would bring her in to talk to the first-year students about being successful when her last marriage turned her into a pariah. There had to be students sitting there with families that suffered because of the horrible things Sawyer King did—and Alexis was by his side while he did most of them.

If I had to sit in a room and pretend like she was some sort of beloved figure after her ex-husband ruined my family, I would probably lose it...

I did my best to focus on my next class. The internal struggle over my relationship with Bryant didn't like being put in the back of my mind, but I needed to pay attention to my professor. He often went on tangents about stuff that wasn't in the textbook, but the information sometimes made a special appearance on the quiz, or in some sort of assignment we had to do. I normally liked that about his class, but my head just wasn't in it. I ended up starting the recorder on my phone just so I wouldn't miss anything.

One quiz isn't going to ruin my GPA, but I still don't want to risk getting a bad grade.

I was ready to scream for joy when the class ended. My eyes were starting to glaze over, and I just needed a break—and another cup of coffee. I had enough time to make a quick trip to the coffee machine, so I started that way. I made it through my entire first year without paying premium price for whatever watered down mess they called coffee, but it wasn't the day to worry about that. I took a sip as I walked towards my class, turned the corner—and nearly ran headfirst into someone that was coming from the opposite direction—except it wasn't just *someone*—it was Alexis Devereaux. I barely came to an abrupt stop—one more step would have left both of us covered in hot coffee.

"I'm sorry, I…" I was mid-apology before I realized who I almost spilled coffee on—unfortunately, none of it actually landed on her.

"Watch where you are going!" She snapped at me, but then her eyes got wide as she realized *who* had almost run her over. "Taylor…you're a student—here…"

"A student that needs to get to class." I didn't know what to do but I wanted to get away from her as soon as possible.

"Not so fast." Alexis caught my arm before I could scramble and caused some of my coffee to spill on my hand.

"Let me go." I shifted my coffee to the other hand and tried to yank my arm free.

"I've been trying to figure out who you were—I was just looking in the wrong place." A shocked—but rather sinister laugh filled the air. "A student? Bryant is dating a student at Carson Cove University—oh this is so fucking rich."

"It doesn't matter who I am." My words seethed across my lips.

"Oh, it matters, darling. It matters a *lot*." She continued laughing but leaned towards me. "Do you even *know* what I can do to a little *nothing* like you?"

"Not a damn thing." My head snapped back.

"I thought you were some socialite—a spoiled little rich girl with a daddy complex. Now I know what's really going on and why nobody could tell me who you were." Alexis shook her head, and the smile immediately turned into a look of pure evil. "You're out of your fucking league."

"Do you really think that? I left on Bryant's arm—you left with your tail tucked between your legs." I tried not to show any signs of weakness, but her words were getting to me, even if I didn't want to admit it.

"Little girls that play with wolves always get eaten." Her eyes reflected disdain for my very existence. "Why don't you just end things with Bryant so that we can put all of this behind us—I'll consider it a lapse of judgment on your part. Otherwise, I'll have to put you in your place, and that won't be pretty —especially now that I know who you really are."

"You don't control my life." My jaw tensed up, and I tried to keep my composure.

"Maybe I should pay a visit to my old friend, Dean Richart. I will know everything there is to know about you in less than an hour—and then you'll regret that day you stumbled into my world. I'm giving you a chance here—*end it*."

"Do you think I'm scared of you?" I leaned forward, but I could feel my knees trying to tremble. "I'm not—I might not come from money, but at least I'm not a stuck up *bitch*."

"Fine. The next time you see me?" Alexis gave me a shove that caused a few people to turn and stare. "You'll be on your knees begging for mercy—and I'll be the one on Bryant's arm. Things are already in motion—but I'm going to enjoy watching you sob when you see just how *fucked* you really are."

Alexis started walking in the opposite direction of the way she was headed when I almost ran into her—she was walking towards Dean Richart's office. My heart sank into my stomach, and I realized that everyone in the hall had witnessed what happened between us—they were staring at me. I couldn't find the strength to go to my next class. I walked to the nearest exit, tossed my coffee in the garbage, and didn't stop walking until I made it to my car.

"Oh my god…" I stared at the steering wheel and tried to process what had just happened.

I had no idea what to do. I didn't want to believe that Alexis Devereaux could ruin my life by talking to Dean Richart —but I had no idea what she was going to tell him. I had worked too hard to have it all come crashing down—and for what? She was mad because Bryant wasn't interested in her? I stepped on her toes when she was trying to hit on him? It wasn't like he would have magically fallen in love with her if I hadn't walked up to them at the art show. Yes, I enjoyed watching someone as privileged as her get shut down while I had a front row seat. I knew I was playing with fire, but I didn't expect her to be the one that burned me.

I should have ended things with Bryant when I had the chance. Now it may cost me everything I've worked for—losing my friendship with Victoria may be the least of my worries...

Chapter Sixteen

BRYANT

*J*had to cancel a few meetings in the morning so I could talk to my lawyer. He advised me not to buy Alcott Inc. The company was in good shape, but it wasn't a great investment—it would be a long time before I recouped the money I spent. It wasn't about that, so I ignored the advice I paid him for, and told him to work with Jon's lawyer to put together a purchase agreement. Mary's lawyer would have to agree to the price—it had to be enough to provide her with a fair compensation. She obviously deserved her share of their accumulated wealth—and it was within her right to ask that assets be liquidated if they couldn't be fairly split—I just hated that their relationship had come down to that.

"Mr. Benson?" Cassie pushed my door open. "Don't forget you have that investor call in ten minutes—Danny Fontenot is already waiting on hold."

"Thanks," I sighed and nodded.

Danny was my newest client, and he seemed to have a very hands-on approach with his investments. There were times when I had my regularly scheduled investor calls and ended up being the only person on the line—most of my clients trusted me or preferred to discuss things in person. Danny had decided to invest in the general fund at Benson Enterprises, which meant the overall health of the company was what turned a profit for him. I still didn't know how he had gained all of his newfound wealth, but that didn't matter—the background check said it was legit, so the rest of it wasn't my business.

The call didn't last long, but two other investors joined Danny for the discussion, and there were a few questions about the fund that I had to answer for them. As soon as the call ended, I saw my phone light up with a message from Victoria.

Victoria: Are you busy?

Bryant: Yes. Shouldn't you be in class right now?

Victoria: One of them got canceled.

Bryant: Ah, okay. Is there a problem, or can this wait until tonight?

Victoria: I just wanted to know if you've talked to Mom recently.

Bryant: No. We don't really talk… Not anymore.

Victoria: You should call her.

Bryant: Why? What's going on?

Victoria: I don't think she's doing well…

Bryant: Dylan said he talked to her recently. Apparently, she has a new job… I think she's fine. You can call her if you think there's a problem.

Victoria: Will you do it? Please? For me?

Bryant: It isn't my place to check in on her anymore. I doubt she wants to hear from me anyway.

Victoria: I still think you should.

I went round-and-round with Victoria, but neither of one of us were saying anything new. It used to be like that when she was a kid—she would just keep making the same request until we gave in or lost our temper and forced her to back off. I had another meeting scheduled, and I couldn't keep playing her game, so I finally just caved. One conversation with my ex-wife wasn't going to kill me, and there was obviously some reason that Victoria thought it was important. I waited until the end of the day to finally pick up my phone, but I didn't dial Sarah's number—there was someone else on my mind, and it sure as hell wasn't my ex-wife.

Bryant: Any chance I can see you tonight?
Taylor: No.
Bryant: Why?
Taylor: Busy with school.
Bryant: Tomorrow?
Taylor: Busy then too.

Taylor's answers were short—and quick. She didn't even think about my request before she declined it. If she was busy with school, I could accept that. I just expected a little more from her response. I thought about addressing my concerns but decided against it. The last thing I wanted was to get into an argument with her, when we could just try to clear the air when we were finally together again. I should have let her say what she had to say when she visited me—I was afraid she was having doubts and tried to erase them. There was a chance it could be something else, and I hoped we could work through whatever it was. I was falling too hard to just let go of her—no matter how complicated our relationship would eventually become.

If I don't have Taylor as an excuse to avoid the phone call, I guess I should call Sarah before Victoria decides to grill me about it.

"Hello?" Sarah's voice echoed on the other end of the line after less than two rings.

"Hey Sarah." I leaned back in my chair. "I—Victoria asked me to call and see if you were okay."

"Why wouldn't I be?" Her tone was rigid, but that was kind of expected—we weren't married anymore.

"I don't know," I sighed. "She must think something is going on."

"I have been meaning to call…" Her tone relaxed.

"Oh?" My eyebrows shot up in surprise.

Maybe Victoria was right…

"It's nothing." The rigidness returned immediately.

"If there's something you want to say to me, just say it. I know we were never very good at this communication thing…" I covered the bottom of my phone and exhaled sharply.

"There's something we should discuss, but it's better if we do it in person," she sighed into the phone.

"Is it about the kids? I know Shaina was off the grid for a little while, but I talked to her—she's fine." I tilted my head slightly and held the phone against my shoulder.

"It's about our family," her voice cracked. "Do you think you could come see me this weekend? I'd come to Carson Cove, but I have to work…"

"Uh…" I stammered over my words as I tried to figure out how to respond.

If I go to the city this weekend, I won't be able to see Taylor —damn it.

"Forget it," she sighed again. "It's not that important."

"If it's about our family, it's important." I leaned forward. "Yeah, I'll come see you this weekend."

"Okay—how about Saturday? Maybe we could meet for lunch?" A hint of hope echoed in her voice—something was definitely *off* in her responses.

"That'll be fine." I waited for her to say something, but she just ended the call.

What the fuck? I don't think she would be so weird about it if she needed to talk to me about the kids…

I wasn't going to get anywhere if I tried to make sense of the conversation, so I just tried to put it in the back of my mind as I drove home. One thought did hit me—there was a chance that she was involved with someone—and wanted to tell me that in person. There was no reason for her to discuss it with me. I certainly had no intentions of telling her about Taylor— even if our relationship wasn't a secret. If that wasn't it, and it wasn't an issue with the kids, then I had no idea what the hell she could want to talk to me about. I wished she would have just told me over the phone, so I didn't have to waste my weekend—and an opportunity to see the woman I was falling for. Our time together was limited enough *without* an unnecessary trip to the city.

At this rate, I may not get to see her until next weekend—that's far too long.

Chapter Seventeen

TAYLOR

The next day

J was terrified to go back to school after my encounter
with Alexis—I was on pins and needles the entire
day. I felt like some of my classmates were staring at me, and I
heard a few whispers that suggested people were talking about
what happened. I was used to being invisible—and I never
wanted to be the center of attention. I made it through two
classes, before Melinda cornered me in the hall—I already
knew what she was going to ask me.

"Hey, Taylor…" She grabbed my arm. "Why are people
talking about you? Did you—get in some kind of argument
with Alexis Devereaux?"

"It was nothing." I shook my head back and forth. "I
almost spilled coffee on her, and she overreacted."

None of that is a lie, but it's not actually connected in any way.

"Ah, okay." She nodded. "Someone said they thought you
were arguing about a guy—I told them they were crazy."

"A guy?" I feigned a confused shrug. "Yeah, that *would* be
crazy…"

Melinda believed it was just a weird rumor that was blown out of proportion by people who misunderstood what they heard. She didn't bring up Bryant's name—which meant *that* part of the conversation didn't register with anyone who saw the exchange. If they had realized I was fighting with Alexis over one of the hottest, richest guys in Carson Cove, then his name would have *definitely* been part of the rumor. I felt a little better when the day ended without incident. I still wasn't taking Alexis' threat lightly, but if there was a problem at school, then Dean Richart would have addressed it immediately.

Maybe Alexis doesn't have the kind of power she thinks—her image is certainly tarnished in Carson Cove after everything that Sawyer King did...

I felt bad about blowing Bryant off when he wanted to see me, and truthfully, I could have gone to see him—but I was terrified of it. I was scared that I wouldn't be able to end things like I wanted—scared that I would wind up in his bed again when it was a mistake. I couldn't shake the feelings that were developing for him, and I hated the thought of ending this after Alexis' threat. I didn't want to give her the perceived satisfaction of being responsible for the end of our relationship. It had to end, no matter what—but she wasn't the reason. I certainly didn't think Bryant was going to fall for her just because our relationship fell apart.

I drove to my house and was surprised to see my mother's car in the driveway. It was unusual for her to make it home before I did. I was normally the first one there, followed shortly by Anna if she didn't have anything going on after school.

"Mom?" I walked into the house and found my mom in the kitchen—with a glass of wine in front of her.

"Hey..." She looked up, and I immediately realized she had been crying.

"What's wrong!?" I dashed to the table and grabbed her hand as I sat down. "Did something happen!?"

"I..." Her voice was shaky, and I saw more tears begin to stream down her face. "I got fired today."

"Are you serious?" I blinked in surprise. "Why?"

"My boss wouldn't tell me..." She reached for her glass of wine and took a sip. "I was walked out by security with no explanation—he said I would be getting a letter from HR."

"He can't do that! They have to tell you what you did..." I shook my head back and forth. "You've been working there your whole life!"

"I felt like some kind of criminal. They wouldn't even let me get my pictures..." She started breaking down, and her words trailed off. "I have no idea what we're going to do."

"We'll be okay." I leaned forward and hugged her. "You'll find something else. I'll get a job to help if I have to—I'm sure Anna can find something after school, even if it's part time."

"No." She shook her head back and forth. "Please don't tell Anna—not yet. I don't want her to worry."

"She's going to be walking in the door any second..." I looked over my shoulder nervously.

"I got a message from her earlier. She's hanging out with friends and won't be home for dinner," my mother sighed.

"Oh..." I nodded. "Mom, we *really* are going to be okay. I know you loved that job, but you've always said you could make more at a bigger company..."

"If they'll hire me... I've been sitting here trying to figure out what I could have possibly done wrong, and I have no idea what it could be. The only time I've seen someone walked out like that was when they were stealing money from the company —I definitely didn't do that!" She shook her head, and I could tell she was on the verge of totally losing it.

"I love you." I leaned over and hugged her. "No matter what..."

I did my best to comfort my mother. All of my problems stopped being important in an instant. It took almost two hours for her to finally calm down and stop crying. She came up with several theories about why she could have been fired, but none of them made sense—and most of them would have been grounds for a lawsuit if it was the real reason her company let her go. Not knowing was the worst part—there was no way that she could figure it out, and I thought the entire situation was bullshit. Being forced to wait on a letter from HR with no real explanation when she was walked out of the building might as well have been torture.

"Do you want me to fix you something to eat?" I put my hand on her arm.

"No, I think I'm just going to go to bed." She finished her wine and leaned forward.

At least she isn't crying anymore…

I didn't have an appetite either, so I decided to hide in my room. If Anna came home, she would see that I was upset and ask questions. I wanted to respect my mother's wishes and if she wanted to wait, then I would let her tell Anna when the time was right—she wouldn't be able to hold off very long. Anna would be curious when our mother didn't go to work the next morning, and she might be able to explain a couple of days away, but eventually it would be too suspicious. I definitely needed to look for a job—there was no way to know how long it would be before my mother was able to find another one.

I won't be able to support our family on my own, but I can help out. I'm sure Anna will want to do the same thing…

The three of us were forced to cling to each other after my father left—and it felt like we were going to have to do it again. We were too strong to give up, or maybe we were just stubborn. It wasn't going to be easy to balance work and school, which is why my parents insisted that I wait until after graduation to start working. My parents never had much compared to the wealthy in Carson Cove, but they were good people—they saved every penny they could so that Anna and I could go to college without having to take out student loans.

I waited until Anna was home before I finally went to bed. I was exhausted from worrying all day about Alexis, and the situation with my mother had left me completely drained, but I wanted to know that my sister was safe. I had just closed my eyes and started to doze when I heard my phone buzz on the table beside me.

I don't recognize this number...

Unknown: Did you enjoy my gift?

Taylor: Who is this?

Unknown: Someone out of your league...

Taylor: Alexis? Why the hell are you texting me?

Unknown: It's rude not to say thank you when you get such an amazing gift.

Taylor: Leave me alone...

Unknown: I thought you would be happy. Your mother will have so much time to spend with you now. Maybe she'll keep you away from men twice your age...

"What the fuck?" I sat up in bed and turned on the light—my stomach immediately started twisting into a knot.

Taylor: You got my mom fired!?! You bitch!

Unknown: You'll get another gift from me tomorrow. If that isn't enough to convince you to end things with Bryant Benson, then my third gift most certainly will...

Taylor: Stay the hell away from me—and my family! I swear to god!

Unknown: I know you're probably thinking that you can run to your sugar daddy and have him fix everything, but that will not end well for you —or your family.

Taylor: What does that mean!?

Unknown: Your sister is such a beautiful girl, isn't she? That boyfriend of hers... Star football player, right?

Taylor: You're a psycho!

Unknown: Goodnight, Taylor. Sweet dreams.

I was so angry that I couldn't even think about going to sleep. Alexis Devereaux got my mother fired—and that was just the beginning of what she planned to do to me if I didn't break up with Bryant. I thought about calling him, but I had no idea what I would say. He couldn't make her back off—and if she found out I went to him for help, she might do something worse—I definitely couldn't risk her doing something to Anna. It wasn't like I could go to the police and show them the text message. I doubted Alexis was stupid enough to use her real phone. She wasn't playing around—she was serious—and her first so-called *gift* was a clear indicator of that. I was definitely out of my league. I couldn't risk my family getting hurt for a guy I should have never gotten involved with in the first place.

I'm sorry, Bryant. I've put this off as long as I can...

The next day

It was almost sunrise when the exhaustion finally forced me to close my eyes—and it felt like only a few minutes passed before my alarm was going off. I went downstairs and made coffee. My mother never came down. Anna asked questions, and all I could do was lie and tell her that mom had the day off. After Anna left for school, I went upstairs and checked on my mother—she wasn't asleep, but she had no interest in getting out of bed. She insisted that I go to school, and while I wanted to stay there with her, I didn't feel like I had much of a choice. I was going to be useless for the entire day, but I had already skipped a few of my classes after my confrontation with Alexis in the hallway—missing more would just put me behind.

My life has turned into a nightmare...

School was a blur—I managed to take a quick nap in my car during the time that I normally had lunch. I wasn't in the mood to eat, so I slept until the phone on my alarm woke me up, and then drank more coffee so I could stay awake for the rest of the day. I had functioned on very little sleep before, but it normally didn't come after an emotionally draining day— nor did I have to spend the whole day worrying about some random second *gift* from Alexis Devereaux. I made it to the last class of the day and was almost home free when my professor called me to his desk—and said that Dean Richart wanted to see me in his office after class.

I have a bad feeling about this—but I can't ignore him...

I felt like was making a walk of shame—or taking my final steps before my execution—when I approached Dean Richart's office. I had never been called to his office before. The only time I had interacted with him was when I was getting an award at the annual assembly. I hoped I wouldn't have any more interactions until I was shaking his hand, the day I got my degree. It was rare for him to meet with a student person- ally—usually the assistant dean handled those meetings—that meant it was either *really* bad, or something totally out of the ordinary.

"I'm here to see Dean Richart." I walked up to his secre- tary's desk, and clutched my purse in my hands.

"Are you Taylor Abernathy?" She looked up at me with a scowl on her face.

"Yes ma'am." I nodded quickly.

"He's waiting for you." She motioned to his office, and it felt like she was staring daggers at me as I walked towards it.

That's definitely not a good sign.

"Dean Richart?" I pushed his door open and felt my stomach twisting into the tightest knot imaginable.

"Taylor Abernathy." His voiced sounded like gravel and the look on his face was far from kind. "Have a seat."

"Yes sir…" I walked over and sat down. "What is this about?"

"I think you know what this is about—I'm just surprised you made it this far without getting caught." He narrowed his eyes.

"I—I have no idea." I tried to swallow a lump that rapidly formed in my throat.

"Plagiarism, Ms. Abernathy." He picked up two sets of papers and threw them down in front of me.

"I've never plagiarized anything!" I shook my head back and forth as panic swept through my veins.

"Then explain how that paper right there has your name on it—and the one next to is from one of those websites where you can buy research papers." He leaned forward. "They're almost identical."

"What!?" I grabbed the first set of papers, which was my assignment, and quickly skimmed it before picking up the other set. "No sir, I didn't plagiarize this. It looks like we used the same sources—but it's an assignment on Picasso. How many sources are there!?"

"Enough for me to believe this is no coincidence." He growled under his breath. "You're suspended—until your academic hearing."

"Dean Richart, I swear! I didn't plagiarize this paper! Please, you have to believe me!" My hands started trembling—my breathing was so hurried it felt like I was going to pass out.

"It'll be up to the academic committee, Ms. Abernathy. We will need a few days to review the rest of your work and see if there are any other instances of plagiarism before we make a final decision, but this is a violation of the honor code." He leaned forward a little more. "It's enough to get you expelled."

"Oh my god…" I felt tears welling up in my eyes.

"That's all, Ms. Abernathy. My secretary will call you when we have a date and time for the hearing—until then, you are not allowed to step foot on campus." He leaned back in his chair.

I wanted to crawl under the chair I was sitting in and die— or fall on my knees and beg Dean Richart for forgiveness— forgiveness for something I didn't even do. I managed to keep my composure long enough to leave his office before the tears started to fall—but I had to walk down the hall in front of the other students with them streaming down my face. It didn't even register until I was outside of the building that my suspension was Alexis Devereaux's second gift—she got my mother fired and she was going to have me expelled from school.

I had no idea how I was going to face my mother and tell her that I had been suspended—or that I was about to be kicked out of school. If Alexis was behind my suspension, then the hearing was just a formality—my time at Carson Cove University had come to an abrupt end. I wasn't going to graduate. I probably wouldn't even be able to find another school to take me—I definitely wasn't going to get credit for any of the classes I had taken that semester, which meant all of the money my parents spent was literally wasted.

My mother doesn't need any more stress—but I can't lie to her...

I walked to my car, and as I approached, I noticed something was wrong—it was tilted to the right. I started walking faster, and when I ran to the passenger side, I got another surprise—probably another gift from Alexis—both of my passenger side tires were flat. There were huge gashes near the wheel where someone had slashed them with a knife. All of my despair just formed a tight ball in my chest—my tears dried up —every bit of emotion left my body, and I just went numb. I opened my driver's side door, sat down in my car, and screamed—I screamed as loud as I could—so loud that people stopped to stare—but I just didn't fucking care.

"You bitch! I fucking hate you! I'm going to fucking kill you, god damn it, I will not…" I threw my head back against the seat and screamed louder—so loud that I didn't even hear my phone buzz, but I saw it light up with a text message.

The same number as last night…

Unknown: Did you enjoy my second gift?

Taylor: Fuck you.

Unknown: That's not very nice.

Taylor: You went too far.

Unknown: Oh? I thought my second gift was quite charming. You'll have plenty of free time to spend with your mother—after you find a way home, of course.

Taylor: Go to hell, you fucking bitch!

Unknown: My third gift will be even better if you don't end things with Bryant.

Taylor: Do you really think that's going to happen now? You got my mother fired. You ruined my life. What do I have to lose at this point? Don't even think about threatening my sister. This is between you and me —and one of us isn't going to see the fucking sun come up.

Unknown: You're such a nasty, horrible girl. It's unladylike.

Taylor: You're going to see how unladylike I can be real soon.

Unknown: End things with Bryant and this will all go away.

Taylor: It's too late for that.

Unknown: No, it isn't. It's just a series of mistakes that can be undone with a couple of phone calls—or they can become permanent mistakes. It's your choice. Do it, or you're going to find out that my third gift is the best one of all.

Taylor: If I end things with Bryant my mother will get her job back?

Unknown: Yes—and she'll get a raise for this terrible misunder-standing.

Taylor: What about school?

Unknown: Another mistake. They'll be eternally grateful for the opportunity to sweep it under the rug once they realize it was their error.

I stared at my phone in disbelief. I had no idea if I could

trust Alexis to undo all of the damage she had done, but if she had the power to cause it—she probably had the power to fix it. My conscious wouldn't let me just ignore her, especially if there was a way to set things right. I could hunt Alexis down— I could pound her face into the pavement—and I would end up in handcuffs—on my way to prison. I wasn't a violent person, even if my rage tried to convince me that I could actually go through with it—all it would do was make things worse. I certainly wasn't going to throw what was left of my life away.

I need to call a tow truck... I only have one spare tire, and that's not enough to get me home.

It took two calls to find a tow truck that could come and get me. The driver was a guy named Steve who tried to make light of the situation, which I really wasn't in the mood for. He changed my good front tire with the bad one in the back so he could tow my car—then let me ride with him to the tire shop. I could only imagine how bad the bill was going to be, but I didn't have much choice except to pay it. Thankfully, he stopped making jokes when he realized how upset I was, and the drive was filled with silence. That was almost worse than his jokes, because I was fighting back tears while seething with rage—neither of which were going to help with the situation at hand, because I already knew what I had to do.

I have to end my relationship with Bryant and pray it's enough to fix the damage it's already caused.

I sat in the waiting area at the tire shop, and my rage finally started to give way to rational thought. As much soul-crushing agony as I was already dealing with, I knew I had to endure one more shattering heartbreak before I could move on. I couldn't go after Alexis on my own—I couldn't let my mother lose her job if there was an option for her to keep it—and I couldn't risk her going after my little sister. There was no doubt in my mind that she would be the next target—and the recipient of Alexis' third gift. Once my car was done, and the bill was paid, I pulled out my phone so I could text Bryant.

Taylor: Hey. Can I stop by?

Bryant: Of course. I would love to see you!

Taylor: On my way…

The tears returned when I started driving to Benson Estate. I was beaten down, destroyed, and my sanity was barely hanging on by a thread. It was going to get worse before I ever got a chance to heal. The memories I had with Bryant flashed through my head like an anguish-filled montage while I drove. I hated every bit of what I had to do, but it was the only path in front of me that made sense. Deep down, I knew it was the right decision, even if it tore me apart to think about it. Saving my friendship with Victoria wasn't even a concern anymore—there was no way I would be able to look her in the eyes or come back to Benson Estate again after I drove Alexis' poisoned dagger through Bryant's heart—then plunged the poison-soaked blade into mine. I couldn't even tell him why—all I could do was lie.

I never belonged in the world of the privileged—so now it's time for me to make my exit.

"I thought I wasn't going to get to see you again until next weekend." Bryant walked out with a smile on his face. "I just found out I have to make a trip to the city—this may be the only chance we get to see each other until then."

The last chance—ever.

"We need to talk." I looked up at him.

"Have you been crying?" He immediately walked over to me. "What's wrong?"

"Don't be nice to me right now…" I rejected his attempt at a hug. "I don't deserve kindness."

"Taylor, talk to me. Whatever is bothering you—we can work through it." He took a step back when he realized I wasn't going to let him hug me.

"No." I shook my head back and forth. "I came here to tell you that it's over."

"Over?" He blinked in confusion. "Why? Are you worried about Victoria? I'm going to talk to her—I know she's your friend and I know it will be complicated, but we have something special. We'll find a way to make her understand…"

"I'm sorry." I looked down. "I've been thinking about it for a while, and I just—I can't be with you. We made a mistake—*I* made a mistake."

I never thought I would call our time together that—but I don't know what else to say.

"Please…" He held up his hands and tried to approach me, but I took a step back. "Don't do this. Tell me what's bothering you and let's talk about it."

"I said what I came to say. Bryant, I'm sorry—it really is over." The tears were coming, so I turned away from him and started walking towards my car.

"Taylor, wait!" He started down the steps after me—and I started running.

I made it to my car before Bryant did, but not quick enough to get my door open. Bryant put his hand on it—and I was forced to look up at him. All of my emotions just flooded out—tears streamed down my face. Bryant pulled me in for a hug, and I didn't have the strength to push him away. His lips found mine, and I melted into that kiss so fast my knees went weak. I was losing the battle again—the battle I absolutely could *not* lose. I just wanted to stay in his arms forever—even if there was a slight chance that we could survive—but I couldn't. I finally found the strength to pull away and get my door open.

"I'm so sorry—I really did care about you. It's just—it won't work." I sat down in my car and Bryant grabbed my door before I could slam it.

"Don't do this, Taylor. I can see it in your eyes—this isn't what you want. Tell me what's really going on." He tightened his grip on my door until his knuckles were white.

"Please…" I started sobbing. "Don't make this any harder than it is."

I pulled on my door until Bryant finally released it. He stared at me with a look of pain and disbelief on his face as I cranked up my car and drove away. I didn't want to go straight home. My mother would be there—and she was dealing with something that would be fixed because I ended things with Bryant. I couldn't hide my emotions from Bryant—I definitely couldn't hide them from her. She was always able to read me like an open book—even when her heart was aching after the divorce. I sent her a quick message to let her know that I wasn't going to be home—I didn't get a response from her, but a few seconds later, my phone lit up with a message from Anna.

Anna: Mom told me.

Taylor: I'm going to be late; can you take care of her tonight?

Anna: Of course.

Taylor: Thank you.

My little sister would never know how close she came to being Alexis Devereaux's next victim—I was going to keep that horrifying reality from her. I hoped it would all be over in a few days, regardless. I wanted to avoid telling my mother about the plagiarism allegation if I could avoid it. I drove around for almost an hour before I finally pulled over on the side of the road. I had a dozen message from Bryant and several missed calls that turned into voicemails. I didn't read or listen to any of them. It was way too hard—I could imagine what they said anyway. I flipped over to the string of messages I had with the unknown number—the one that obviously belonged to Alexis, even if she had never said so.

Taylor: It's over.

Unknown: Good. You made the right decision.

"No… I made the only one I could." I squeezed my phone

in my hand so tight it felt like it was about to crack. "Now I have to find a way to live with it."

The decision that will probably become my biggest regret one day—because I lost the man that stole my heart before I even realized he was doing it.

Chapter Eighteen

BRYANT

The next day

"Cancel all of my fucking meetings." I grabbed my cup of coffee from Cassie and immediately threw it in the garbage.

"Mr. Benson, what's wrong?" Cassie looked at me in confusion.

"Did I stutter?" I growled at her. "Cancel them."

"Yes sir." She nodded and ran to her desk.

I was in a foul mood, and I couldn't help it. I barely got any sleep—I did need coffee, but it would give me a buzz, and the only thing I wanted to feel was the shredded nothingness inside me. I had no idea why Taylor ended our relationship. There were plenty of reasons that made sense, but she didn't tell me which one caused her to bring an abrupt end to what was blooming into something beautiful between us. All I could do was accept her decision and move on—there were no other choices on the table. She wasn't returning my calls. She didn't answer my texts. I couldn't exactly show up on her doorstep with a bouquet of flowers in my hand and my heart on my sleeve.

"Mr. Benson, I'm sorry…" Cassie pushed my door open and quickly apologized.

"For what?" I stared at her in confusion. "I don't want to be disturbed."

"This won't take long." A voice echoed behind Cassie—and then I watched Alexis Devereaux shove my secretary out of the way. "Get lost."

"Mr. Benson, should I call security?" Cassie regained her composure without falling—which was surprising considering how hard Alexis slammed into her.

"No," I exhaled sharply. "Leave us."

"You need better help." Alexis slammed the door as soon as Cassie was gone.

"What the hell do you want Alexis? You're the last person I want to see right now." I glared at her.

"Word on the street is that your relationship with your little tramp is over." She narrowed her eyes at me.

"How the fuck do you know that?" I tensed up.

"It's not important—what is important is why I'm here." She walked over and sat down. "Let's talk business."

"I don't do business with you," I growled under my breath. "Never have—never will."

"Today you will." She smiled. "Unless you want me to give you a gift."

"A gift?" I scoffed and shook my head. "I don't want shit from you—but I do want you to go."

"Not even this gift?" Alexis pulled a tablet out of her purse and turned it towards me as she hit play.

I stared at the screen and tried to make sense of what I was seeing. It was a room—I could see a table, a couple of chairs, a couch, and a television. I had no idea why it was important. A couple of seconds later, I watched someone walk into view. It was a large, muscular guy that wasn't wearing a shirt. He had a lot of ink, but it wasn't classy—it looked like the kind of ink people got in prison.

There was a woman on the edge of the screen, but all I could see was her leg. The guy held up a baggie with white powder—cocaine or heroin, I wasn't sure which. He poured some on the table, chopped it up—and snorted it through a straw. He handed the straw to the woman and leaned back as she leaned forward—then I realized who it was—I watched my oldest daughter snort a line of white powder big enough to make an addict cringe.

"What the fuck is this?" I grabbed the tablet out of Alexis' hand and stared at the video in horror.

"It's a gift." She motioned to the tablet. "Like I said…"

"How the hell did you get this video?" I slammed the tablet down hard enough to crack the screen. "Answer me!"

"So—violent." Alexis' head snapped back. "We'll have to work on that temper after we're married."

"Married?" I scoffed. "I asked you a question."

"I came across it." She shrugged. "Someone thought that a video of Bryant Benson's oldest daughter doing drugs would be worth something—it was. I now have the only copy."

"You want money? Fine. Name your fucking price…" I glared at her.

"My price is simple. Marry me. The video will be my wedding present to my new husband." She smiled and nodded.

"You're fucking insane." I shook my head back and forth. "I have to go."

"If you walk out of this office without giving me what I want, that video will be all over the Internet tonight—everyone in Carson Cove will know your daughter is a drug addict—and isn't she in law school? I'm pretty sure that would cause problems…" She shrugged.

"This is your copy?" I grabbed the tablet and started smashing it on the desk, then hurled it against the wall.

"I mean, obviously it's stored in my cloud—but you owe me a tablet now." She narrowed her eyes and stared at me.

"So, you're blackmailing me?" I leaned forward and did my best to stare a hole through the bitch in front of me. "You want me to marry you so that this video doesn't get out?"

"Yes." She nodded. "That's it—exactly."

"You really are insane." I shook my head back and forth. "I need to go take care of my daughter—and figure out what the hell is going on with her."

"Okay." She nodded. "I'll give you a few days to decide— the video will be safe with me until then. See, I'm not so bad— I'm giving you an extension."

"I…" There was a lot I wanted to say. "I'll talk to you when I get back."

I went my whole life without having true hatred for another human being. I got angry with them—I was certainly angry at Sarah when she left—but I never hated her. Hate was a strong word—but that's the only thing I felt towards Alexis Devereaux as I stormed out of my office and headed to the car. I booked my flight on the way to the airport, sent a message to Cassie to let her know that I would be away for a few days, and made it to the terminal with an hour to kill before my flight left Carson Cove. My mind started to process everything—and I immediately began to think about my conversation with Sarah. I pulled out my phone and dialed her number.

"Hello?" Sarah's voice echoed on the other end of the line.

"Hey—this thing you wanted to talk to me about. Did it have something to do with Shaina?" I exhaled sharply.

"It—it isn't something I want to discuss over the phone." Her tone was hurried. "I'm at work right now."

"Well I just saw a video—a really bad one," I growled under my breath. "Did you know she's using drugs!?"

"What?" I could tell by her reaction that she didn't. "No! I knew something was going on with her—that's why I wanted to talk to you. I thought it was something we needed to address as a family, but I had no idea it was drugs! Bryant, oh my god. Are you sure?"

"Yes, I'm absolutely positive." I shook my head angrily.

"I just—I thought it was stress or something. I was afraid we had put too much pressure on her and she..." Sarah hesitated for a moment.

"She what?" I walked close to the window and leaned against it.

"She told me that she was having second thoughts about being a lawyer." Sarah's voice cracked, and it sounded like she was about to start crying. "She didn't want to say anything to you because you were so proud of her..."

"Fuck me..." I put my hand on the window and resisted the urge to punch it. "Okay, I'm at the airport. I'm going to see her. I'll call you when I know something."

"Bryant..." I could hear a sob echoing in Sarah's throat. "Please take care of our baby."

"I will..." I pulled the phone away from my ear and ended the call.

Sarah may not have loved me anymore, but she still loved our children. The divorce didn't change that—nothing could. It's why I could never find it in my heart to hate her. I walked over to one of the seats in the terminal and sat down. It felt like my life was falling apart. My relationship with Taylor was obviously over. My daughter was on drugs. The cherry on top—the disgusting, rotten cherry—was Alexis Devereaux's proposal. If you could even call it that. She controlled my daughter's future, and the only way I was going to be able to keep the video from seeing the light of day was to enter into unholy matrimony with her.

She sure as fuck went to a lot of trouble just to pillage half of my fortune—but I think she's won this battle. Shaina's young and she can overcome this, but that video could ruin her damn life—even if she doesn't want to be a lawyer.

I stared at the wall and seethed until it was time for me to board my plane. I rarely flew first class, even though I could afford it, but I simply didn't want to be bothered by anyone unless it was absolutely necessary. I knew the people in first class would ignore me—and as luck would have it—there weren't many people flying up front. I got a drink as soon as it was offered and sipped it slowly while I watched the clouds go by. My phone connected to the Wi-Fi and immediately lit up with a message from Cassie. I had an email from my lawyer—it was the purchase agreement for Alcott Inc.

Mary's lawyer accepted the proposal. All I have to do is sign some paperwork to make it official—but that could be a problem if I'm forced to marry Alexis.

I had no doubt that if Alexis' motivation was money, she would have her lawyers tear into my assets to make sure she got a shot at everything when she was ready to cash out of the marriage. My agreement with Jon would be worthless—hell, she could pull the same shit his wife pulled and force me to sell Benson Enterprises. I wasn't going to have enough liquid capital to avoid that after I bought Alcott Inc. Benson Enterprises was worth too much, and *all* of my investments were in the general fund. I was fucked no matter which way I turned, and it could bring Jon down too. I couldn't do that to him after giving him a semblance of hope.

Maybe hate isn't a strong enough word for how I feel about Alexis Devereaux. That bitch is the devil incarnate...

Chapter Nineteen

TAYLOR

I stayed out as late as possible after breaking up with Bryant. I came home after everyone was in bed. I was so exhausted that I collapsed into a dark, dreamless sleep. I woke up the next morning to a little bit of chaos that made me temporarily forget what was going on inside me. My mother got a call from her old boss and he told her that there had been a mistake—or a misunderstanding as he put it. She was cleared to return to work immediately, which meant she had to scramble to get ready. Anna and I let her get ready first, and then we rushed to get ready after she was done. I was just pretending—because I didn't have anywhere to go. I made a deal with the devil, and the rewards were already coming my way—if I could even call them that. One wrong was put right —at least my mother was happy.

"Okay, I have to go." My mother looked around the kitchen.

"Good luck, Mom." I walked up and hugged her.

"Thank you." She smiled and nodded.

"I'm glad everything worked out." Anna hugged her as soon as she took a step back from my embrace.

"It's about time for you to go to school too isn't it?" I gave Anna a nudge as our mother rushed to the door.

"Yeah, I guess so," she sighed and grabbed her backpack.

As soon as they were gone, the emotions caught back up with me. I sat down at the kitchen table and started crying. My future hadn't been fixed yet. I had to hold onto the bit of hope that it would be. Alexis rectified the situation with my mother —that was a good start. I drank a cup of coffee and tried to figure out what I was going to do since I didn't have to go to school. The tears didn't last long—I think I was all cried out at that point. I was still trying to decide between moping around and trying to watch a movie on Netflix when my phone started ringing, and I saw that it was from Carson Cove University.

"Hello?" I lifted the phone to my ear.

"Ms. Abernathy? This is Dean Richart," a gravelly voice echoed on the other end of the line.

"Yes sir..." I couldn't help but hesitate—I had no idea why he was calling—he said I would get a call from his secretary, so I wasn't expecting to hear from him directly.

"I just wanted to let you know that your hearing is at noon. We are done with our investigation and we'll review your case —your attendance is required," he exhaled sharply.

"Of course, absolutely." I felt a glimmer of hope as I replied.

Maybe my situation is going to be resolved today as well...

Later that day

I arrived at Carson Cove University thirty minutes before my hearing was scheduled to start. It was being held in one of the small assembly rooms—ironically enough, the same one where Alexis Devereaux gave her speech to the first-year law students. I assumed that word about my suspension hadn't leaked—otherwise Melinda would have been blowing up my phone. I wasn't ready to believe that the situation was going to be fully resolved until I heard the academic committee's ruling—there was a chance that I could still be expelled. Alexis' word didn't mean much to me, even if she did fix things with my mother's job.

"Ah, you're here." Alexis turned the corner, and her face lit up when she saw me—a stark contrast to our previous encounters.

"I am—but why are you?" I raised my eyebrows inquisitively as rage started to flood my veins.

"I'm just here to observe the hearing." She smiled. "I want to make sure Carson Cove University's brightest young art student gets treated fairly."

"I did what you asked—what more do you want from me?" I narrowed my eyes and tried to control my anger.

"Nothing. Our business is done." She walked to the assembly room and opened the door.

Alexis was talking to Dean Richart when I was finally summoned—and the hearing was a complete joke. The academic council had already made their decision and rendered it less than ten minutes after I walked in. It was a terrible mistake, there was no plagiarism, and they were dropping the suspension. I would be allowed to make up any work that I missed, and they were giving me an extension on all of my assignments. I would have been happy under normal circumstances, but the entire ordeal left me sick to my stomach. I didn't do anything wrong, but my entire future could have been ruined by one wave of Alexis Devereaux's greedy finger.

"I trust this will be the last time we see each other." Alexis walked up to me outside to assembly room once the hearing was over.

"You never know. I might come to the wedding just so I can see if he'll really say *I do*." I narrowed my eyes at her.

"Oh, he will. Bryant and I discussed it earlier this morning." She held up her hand. "I already have an engagement ring."

"What the hell…" I blinked in surprise.

"Well, I picked it out myself, and he hasn't seen it yet—but I charged it to his account at Mancini Jewelers. I know he'll approve the charge." She smiled. "Bryant will obviously want his new bride to have the best ring in Carson Cove."

"You win, Alexis." I shook my head back and forth. "I'm going home."

"Hold on—you made a good point. You definitely should be at the wedding…" She tapped her finger on her chin. "I know! You can be my Maid of Honor!"

"No thank you." I felt my rage returning.

"Oh, but I insist." Her smiled turned into the sinister one I remembered. "You should right there by my side when he says his vows—it's only right since you were instrumental in making the big day possible. If you decline, I'll just have to find you a wonderful gift…"

Great, she's still threatening me…

"Fine." I gritted my teeth and did everything I could to resist the urge to slap the lipstick off her face.

"I thought you would be honored to stand by my side." Alexis nodded and started walking towards the door. "I'll have my people call your people—or I'll just text you…"

Alexis had won another battle—I was powerless to do anything to stop her. The reset button on my life had officially been pressed, and I had to find a way to make it worth living—without Bryant. I wondered if he had any idea that our relationship came to a crashing halt because of his bride-to-be. It was too risky to tell him. I had to stand in the world of the privileged one final time while he said his vows to the most awful woman on the planet—and then I would be permanently done with their world. I didn't belong there—I didn't even think I was going to stay in Carson Cove after graduation. The open wound would never heal if I didn't leave—somewhere out there was a future that I could embrace—I just had to find it first.

I can't stop any of this, so I might as well move on. What choice do I have?

Chapter Twenty

"Shaina, open up." I knocked on my daughter's door—I didn't know if she was inside, but I was going to break the door down if I had to.

"Who's there?" A rather gruff voice answered.

"Open the fucking door." I knocked louder.

"Dad? Dad is that you? Hold on!" I heard Shaina's hurried voice on the other side of the door.

I had been in town for a couple of hours, but Shaina's apartment wasn't my first stop. I went to the university and spoke with the dean first—he was hesitant to tell me anything until he realized my name was on all of the tuition checks he was cashing—he got real friendly after that. Shaina was barely scraping by academically. She was attending most of her classes, but there had been a clear downward spiral over the last year. He introduced me to a few of her professors who confirmed the same thing.

I didn't tell them that my daughter was using drugs, but I got the impression that they knew *something* was wrong. They had noticed a personality shift—and she wasn't hanging around the same people she had called friends for a couple of years. She had become quite a loner inside the classroom—but I knew that wasn't the case outside of it. The guy in the video didn't look like a student at *any* school, much less an Ivy League one.

"Open the door—now!" I was two seconds away from putting my boot through it.

"What are you doing here?" Shaina cracked the door—she had large, dilated pupils that confirmed she was high as a fucking kite.

"Figuring out what the hell is going on." I pushed the door open and barged into her apartment.

"Hey, what the fuck?" The guy she was with was the one from the video—and he was a *lot* bigger than I realized.

"I'm going to have a talk with my daughter—alone." I narrowed my eyes. "Get the hell out of here."

"You're the one that needs to go, old man," he growled and took a step forward.

I didn't see the punch coming until my ears were ringing and my head was spinning—he hit me so damn hard that I was pretty sure I had a concussion the second his enormous fist slammed into my skull. It had been a long damn time since I took a punch—but he didn't hit me hard enough to knock me out completely, and that was the last mistake he got to make. I managed to duck his next punch, drive my shoulder into his midsection, and deliver an uppercut that staggered him. Somewhere in the midst of it all, Shaina screamed—and tried to get in the middle of us.

The mother fucker that hit me pushed her so hard she went tumbling over the coffee table and hit her head on the way down. I saw blood on the floor—which meant I had to end the fight and take care of her—but her boyfriend, or whatever the hell he was, didn't seem to give a damn about the fact that he hurt her. He swung at me—I ducked. He tried to hit me with a knee on the way up—I barely dodged that one, but I caught his leg and got him down to the floor. He landed hard—and a few punches to his face kept him down.

"Shaina are you okay? Oh god..." I scrambled to her side and saw a gash that was pouring blood. "We need help! Anyone!?"

The fight brought some other residents from their apartments to see what the commotion was—there were several witnesses in the hallway. One of them called 911. I did my best to contain the bleeding and keep her awake as we waited on the paramedics to arrive. The sirens brought her behemoth of a boyfriend back to life, and when he realized the cops were in the building, he took off. The cops had me in handcuffs the second they entered the apartment—it obviously looked like I was the one who was responsible for the bleeding girl on the floor and the carnage. I was taken to a squad car—my daughter was taken to an ambulance. I sat there stewing for nearly twenty minutes before someone finally opened the back door.

"Okay, Mr. Benson." The cop reached in and pulled me out and turned me around so he could remove the handcuffs. "We talked to some of the witnesses in the apartment building—you're free to go."

"I'm glad to see that defending my daughter isn't a crime." I rubbed my wrists and glared at him.

"If the guy decides to press charges, you might be hearing from us again." He put his hands on his hips.

"I don't think you're going to be hearing from him," I growled under my breath and started walking towards my car.

There was no mention of drugs. Either they got hidden when they realized I was at the door, or the guy took them when he fled. That was something of a blessing. I drove straight to the hospital and found out that Shaina was still being checked out by the doctor—and they would probably keep her overnight for observation. *They* definitely noticed she was high, so that was an obvious concern. The doctor came to see me after they did a CT scan and said she had a nasty cut that required a few stitches but, she didn't have a skull fracture or a brain injury. Keeping her overnight was just a formality. That was a relief—if there was one in that situation.

The doctor said I would be able to see her in a couple of hours, so I called Sarah while I waited. Sarah told me that she was going to fly out immediately, and while I didn't think that was entirely necessary, I couldn't tell the mother of my child that she shouldn't come—not when her daughter was in the hospital. I waited until Shaina was moved to a room, and then the ER nurse gave me a pass so I could go up to her floor. Seeing my daughter in a hospital bed with blood on the bandage they had put on her head made me want to break down in tears, but I did my best to fight them.

"Dad…" Shaina's face got red, and she started crying the minute she saw me at her door. "I'm so sorry."

"You shouldn't try to talk—just rest for now." I walked into the room and sat down beside her bed.

"That's going to leave a mark." She reached out and touched the spot on the side of my face—I could already tell I was going to have a black eye and bruising halfway down my face. "Did the doctor's look at it?"

"Please…" I pushed her hand away. "Don't worry about me. Just rest…"

I wasn't sure if the doctors had given Shaina something for the pain or opted not to since she was high when the paramedics brought her in, but she was definitely out of it. That could have been the result of losing blood. She was stable—that was all that mattered. She tried to talk for a couple of minutes before she finally closed her eyes. The smart thing would have been for me to go back to the ER and have them check me out—my vision was a little blurry and head was throbbing. I got a couple of concussions on the football field when I was younger, and I definitely had one, but it was pretty mild. I didn't lose consciousness, and I wasn't throwing up—I had done both when I got knocked for a loop in high school, and they didn't do anything but put some smelling salts under my nose before they put me back in the game.

I can add getting my skull smashed by a coke head to the list of accomplishments I thought I'd never have.

"Is she resting?" The door to Shaina's room opened, and a nurse walked in.

"Yeah." I nodded. "Is it safe for her to sleep with a head injury?"

"The doctor said it would be fine—we did give her something to help her rest after he gave the okay." She picked up Shaina's chart, flipped through it, and checked the monitors. "Did the doctor tell you what showed up in her blood test?"

"He did," I sighed.

Cocaine...

"I'll check back in a couple of hours." She walked around the bed and patted my shoulder. "I've been through this with my own daughter. I know it's hard."

"Yeah..." I sighed again.

"You should really get that looked at." She motioned to the side of my face. "You may have a fracture hiding under all of that bruising."

"I'll be okay." I looked up at her and forced a smile.

I stayed by Shaina's side until Sarah arrived—and there was a whole lot of crying when she saw her daughter—followed by concern for the way my face looked. Sarah wouldn't let me brush off her concern, and I learned a long time ago that her stubbornness was worse than mine. I ended up back in the ER, waiting to see a doctor, while she sat with our daughter. My injury wasn't serious, and nothing was broken, but it was pretty clear that I had a concussion. I got a lot of literature about what I should do when I got home and a prescription for pain pills I would never get filled. Sarah met me in the emergency room as soon as I was released.

"There, they confirmed I'm not going to die." I walked up to her and sighed.

"How did we screw this up so badly?" Sarah's eyes filled with tears, and she grabbed me for a hug.

I didn't return her hug at first—it was a little painful to have her arms wrapped around me after she walked out on our marriage. I finally succumbed and hugged her while she cried on my shoulder. I tried to reassure her, but I had too many concerns of my own to ease hers. We decided to spend the night in Shaina's room so we would be there when she woke up. At some point, we had to have a very serious conversation, but I wasn't sure when that would be. I wasn't sure if the drugs had a grip on her or if she was just in the recreational stage— but it was clear that she needed help. If she didn't want to be a lawyer, then she didn't have to be—I had to be the one to tell her that I was proud of her no matter what she did with her life—as long as she got off the drugs. The next few days were going to be trying for our family.

Hopefully I can convince her to move back to Carson Cove, and take some time to recuperate before she decides what she wants to do next.

A few days later

Shaina was released from the hospital and after a long discussion, she agreed that she should spend thirty days in rehab just to be safe. She wasn't having withdrawals or showing any serious signs of addiction, but she needed a fresh start. We got her set up with a facility in the city, and Sarah said she would check on her daily. We talked with Victoria and Dylan to let them know what was going on. Dylan said he would check in with Shaina as often as he could, and Victoria was ready to book a flight home, but I convinced her to wait—it wasn't like she could do anything if she was there, and she needed to focus on school. I stayed behind for an additional day to handle things at the university and pack up her apartment.

After that, it was time for me to return to Carson Cove—and the next chapter of my fucked up life. I did my best to handle things remotely when I could while I was away, but there was one problem I would have to handle face-to-face—the biggest problem of all. I had to figure out what the fuck I was going to do about Alexis, but she wasn't the woman I started texting when I boarded the plane—there was someone else on my mind that I just didn't know how to stop thinking about.

Bryant: I know you don't want to hear from me right now, but I miss you...

Taylor: Please don't say that.

Bryant: Why? Do you miss me too?

Taylor: It's over, Bryant. What we had was special, but—we knew it wasn't going to last.

Bryant: Why?

Taylor: It was too complicated.

Bryant: We knew the risk. We decided to take it. I don't regret a single second, and neither should you.

Taylor: I'm sorry. Please don't contact me again. That will make it easier for both of us...

Bryant: If that's what you really want.

Taylor didn't respond—that was her answer. It truly was over. There was no way to repair whatever had torn us apart, and I still didn't understand what that was. Alexis was waiting on me when I arrived at Benson Enterprises, and my willpower was shattered. I didn't have an ounce of fight left in me. I agreed to marry her in order to protect my daughter, even though I had no idea if the video would actually harm her—I just wanted it to go away. The faster I married Alexis, the faster we could get divorced, but I had a lot of shit to figure out before she got her claws in the money she was after.

"Hey, Cassie." I walked to the door after Alexis was gone.

"Yes sir?" Cassie looked up at me.

"I need you to set up a meeting for me—Addison Regan. This one doesn't need to go on my calendar. Just text me the information…" I exhaled sharply.

"Sir? She's not one of your clients—or one of our attorneys." Cassie tilted her head in confusion.

"I know." I closed my door and walked back to my desk.

That's the fucking point.

Chapter Twenty-One

TAYLOR

Several days later

"Ⓘt looks like you might get to see Victoria soon." My mother looked up from the table as I walked into the kitchen.

"What do you mean?" I tensed up immediately.

"Her father is getting remarried." She pushed the newspaper to the edge of the table. "Alexis Devereaux—I never thought *those* two would end up together."

If you only knew half of it...

"Yeah." I shrugged. "Victoria told me they were getting married..."

That's true, but I knew long before I got that frantic text message from my best friend—and I still didn't know how I was going to explain why I was the Maid of Honor.

Victoria wasn't going to wait until the wedding to return to Carson Cove. She was probably already at the airport waiting for her plane to take off. She had tried to talk some sense into her father over the phone, and after that didn't work, she decided that she was going to pay him a personal visit. I knew it was as losing fight—even if I didn't know why. Alexis had *something* on him—and it was probably similar to what she did to me in order to end our relationship. There was no way he would have ever agreed to marry her on his own.

I was just stumbling around an inferno, and my clothes were already on fire—eventually it was going to consume me entirely. Even if Victoria never found out about my relationship with her dad, she would see my willingness to be the Maid of Honor as a betrayal—and she would demand answers—and I couldn't even come up with a lie that made sense.

One final nail through my heart, courtesy of Alexis Devereaux...

It was Saturday, so I had nowhere to be—I would have much rather been at school. At least that would have given me a distraction from everything. Things were better at home after my mother got her job back—and it came with a sizable raise, just like Alexis said. In fact, my mother was talking about buying Anna a car—which made her ecstatic. Everyone in the Abernathy household was happy except me. I was dying a slow death with each passing day.

"I've got a few errands to run. Do you want to come with me?" My mother leaned back in her chair.

"I—I think I'm just going to stay here today," I sighed. "I've got some school stuff to catch up on."

I'd rather wallow in my misery than pretend to be happy...

"Okay." She nodded. "I won't even bother to ask Anna. I know she won't go."

My mother left, and I sat down to have a cup of coffee. I couldn't even imagine what Bryant was going through, and it tore me up that I couldn't be there to support him. During one of my conversations with Victoria, she told me about her sister, which added another horrible gash to my gushing heart. That probably shredded Bryant worse than the end of our relationship and his impending married to Alexis. I didn't know if he had figured out that Alexis was responsible for what happened between us, but *something* happened—or he would have never agreed to marry the bitch.

"I fucking hate you..." I muttered under my breath, picked up the wedding announcement, and started tearing it to pieces.

"Me?" Anna walked into the kitchen and seemed startled by what she heard—and what she saw.

"No." I stood up and dumped my coffee in my sink.

I ran upstairs before Anna could ask another question. I didn't mean for her to see how upset I was—and I definitely didn't intend for her to walk in on me destroying the wedding announcement. My emotions just got the best of me. I needed an outlet and screaming wasn't an option with her in the house, so I put a canvas up and started attacking it with my brush. I a few crimson slashes, outlined those in black, and used the brightest red I could find to draw a heart around them. I was just about to start filling it in when I heard my door open—I knew it was Anna—the footsteps were too soft to belong to my mother.

"You're painting again..." Anna walked in and closed the door.

"Yeah," I sighed. "I don't even know why."

"Do you want to talk about it." She walked up beside me and put her hand on my arm.

"I—no..." I felt tears welling up in my eyes.

"We used to be so close—I know I'm still a kid, but I do have an ear." He put her head against my shoulder. "You're going to through something—something bad..."

Tears started streaming down my face, and Anna hugged me. An emotional valve just turned on—and kept turning until it was wide open. I started telling Anna everything. It was foolish—those secrets should have gone to the grave with me— but they wanted to be let out in a mixture of tears and sobs. Anna listened, hugged me, and listened some more—until she was all caught up on her big sister's mistakes. I couldn't believe

I was spilling my darkest secrets to a sixteen-year-old girl, but she just happened to have the right ear at the right time.

"We can't let her do this to you." Anna squeezed my hand. "Alexis Devereaux has to be stopped..."

"Did you miss the part about *you* being the next one to get one of her horrible gifts?" I wiped away my tears. "She's cruel and heartless—I don't even want to think about what lengths she would really go to."

"Screw her—no, *fuck* her." Anna pulled away and stood up —it was the first time I had ever heard my little sister curse. "We'll stop the wedding! We'll expose her!"

"Don't you think I haven't considered it?" I looked up at Anna. "I was ready to drive to her house on two good tires and beat the makeup off her face—but what good would it do? She'll ruin my life if I try anything, and if I lay a hand on her —I'll just end up in handcuffs."

"We need to call Victoria as soon as she's in Carson Cove." Anna nodded. "She needs to know the truth."

"Oh god no." I shook my head back and forth. "I can't tell her—*I'll* be the one getting the makeup beaten off my face. If she even thinks I'm worthy of a slap after she hears what I've done..."

"She's going to find out eventually, right?" Anna sat back down. "Think about it—you're the damn Maid of Honor, sis. She's not going to believe that you're there because you want to be. Do you think she'd rather hear whatever crap Alexis comes up with to explain it, or the truth from you?"

"She would probably prefer a lie..." I looked down. "I would..."

"No, you wouldn't. I want you to actually think about that. The role is reversed. You just found out Victoria has been in the city having sex with dad—okay, don't picture it, just go with what I'm saying. What would you do?" She squeezed my hand.

"I would be angry..." I stared at the wall. "Really angry..."

"Why?" Anna tilted her head to the side.

"It's my dad." I looked down for a moment.

"Would you end your friendship with her? Would you *hate* her?" Anna leaned forward until she was able to look me in the eye. "What if they were in love?"

"I..." A lump formed in my throat, and I swallowed it. "I would be upset, but I would try to accept it."

"Why do you think Victoria would have a different reaction?" Anna shrugged. "Seriously, think about it."

I didn't have an answer. From the lips of my little sister came the harshest truth I needed to hear. My friendship with Victoria was either going to end or it wasn't—lying wasn't going to change it. Either she found out that I had been involved with her father and hated me for that or hated me for standing at his venomous bride's side—unless she was willing to forgive me. She would probably forgive me for the relationship with her father a lot faster than she would forgive me for choosing Alexis over her—that's what it would ultimately come down to. That would be her perception, no matter what.

"Can we call Victoria?" Anna gave me a slight nudge.

"Yeah, I think we have too..." I exhaled sharply.

Victoria might have had hopes of her parents reconciling at some point, but that was off the table completely. The only hope we had of possibly stopping the wedding was figuring out what Alexis had on Bryant—Victoria would have access—she might even be able to get her father to tell her the truth. My relationship with Bryant was ruined—I didn't think we could salvage it, regardless of what happened in the end, but if there was a way to stop Alexis from carving her way through his empire, then I owed him that much. We just had to find a way to nullify Alexis—or expose her for the heartless bitch she truly was. She had too much power in Carson Cove for me to do that on my own, but Victoria was a different story. Whether she liked it or not, she was one of the privileged—she had resources.

"Victoria?" I tried to hold back my emotions. "Are you in Carson Cove yet?"

"No, my flight got delayed. I won't be there until tonight." I heard a sharp inhale, then a loud exhale. "This is so frustrating!"

"I'm sorry." I looked at Anna, and she motioned for me to keep going—she probably realized I was close to chickening out. "Hey, when you get here. Can you come by my house first? I have something to tell you—it's about Alexis Devereaux—and your father."

"You can't tell me on the phone?" Her tone reflected a hint of annoyance. "I really want to see my dad as soon as possible."

"Trust me, you'll want to hear what I have to say first—and it's gotta be done in person." I felt another lump and tried to swallow it.

"Okay, I'll let you know when I land…" Her voice trailed off. "Hey, it looks like they're about to give us an update—maybe they got me on another flight. I gotta go."

All I can do now is wait…

---

*V*ictoria wasn't able to get on an earlier flight, so it was already dark before her plane touched down in Carson Cove. My mother had a date—which was fortunate since I didn't want her to be there when I talked to Victoria. Anna agreed to stay in her room but threatened to come down the stairs with a baseball bat if Victoria tried to hurt me—I didn't think it would come to that. Truthfully, if she wanted to hit me—I would just have to take it. I was pretty sure she would storm out before she would take a swing, but either option would be understandable. There were some things that were just unforgivable—even if she didn't turn anger into hatred.

"She's here…" I looked over at Anna.

"Okay, I'll be upstairs—waiting." She narrowed her eyes and squeezed my hand before she walked away.

I couldn't lay the news on Victoria immediately. There were hugs to be exchanged and happy smiles to go along with our reunion. Mine was fake—hers looked like it took a lot of effort to muster. I didn't think she would have a smile on her face much longer, not when I hit her with the truth. I tried to stay pleasant as I prepared to execute our friendship in the middle of my living room. I offered her a drink—she accepted —that gave me a few more minutes to spare as I went to the kitchen and poured some wine. I decided to bring the bottle— one more thing that she could hit me with if she raged.

"Alright, tell me what you couldn't tell me on the phone." She sat down on the couch and sipped her wine. "Or were you just looking for an excuse to see me before I went protective daughter-zilla on Alexis Devereaux?"

"I wish…" I looked down and sighed. "There's something I really need to tell you."

I started at the beginning. I told her about the art show— seeing Alexis with her father—and pretending to be his date. The concern began to register on her face, especially when I told her about the auction and the kiss that was supposed to be so innocent. I didn't even know if that was a lie—I was attracted to him then—he was attracted to me. She finished her glass of wine when I told her about our first date—and poured another one as what looked like rage started to form in her eyes. I left out the intimate details. She could obviously fill that part in without me saying it. That was as far as I got before she interrupted me.

"You were the mystery woman..." She shook her head back and forth and her hand squeezed the wine glass so hard I thought it was going to break.

"I—yes." I looked down and nodded. "I swear I was going to end it with him after you told me that your parents might get back together..."

"It was never going to happen. My mother was worried about my sister—anyway, keep going. I should hear it all before I lose my fucking mind." She seemed to be holding her rage in check, which was surprising.

I told Victoria about Alexis—how she blackmailed me—and how that put me in a tough spot when I already knew I needed to end things. That seemed to intensity Victoria's rage, because she quickly started to put together the same pieces I had—her father was a victim of blackmail too. It was the only reason he would have agreed to marry a despicable bitch like Alexis Devereaux. All I could do was finish my story and let her seethe—which she did—without saying a word. The silence was scarier than having her lash out at me, because I had no idea what was going on in her head.

"Did you love him?" She narrowed her eyes.

"I—I honestly don't know." I looked down. "I really cared about him—I still do. It was... What we had was special—that's the only way I can explain it. I knew it was wrong, but I was in over my head before I realized I was drowning."

"Because he's amazing..." Victoria exhaled sharply. "Any woman would be lucky to have him—except the one who currently does."

"I agree. I didn't tell you because I want you to accept the relationship—nor do I think we're going to get back together if he doesn't marry Alexis. I just wanted you to know what you were dealing with before you walked into the venomous bitch's lair." I felt tears welling up in my eyes, and I didn't know how to stop them.

"I'm angry—I'm very angry at you." She took a drink of her wine. "But I'm fucking *pissed* at Alexis Devereaux, so right now, it's a good thing you're the only one in the room."

"I'm sorry, Victoria..." My tears were followed by a sob.

"Don't be sorry." She shook her head back and forth. "We're going to make *her* sorry—she messed with my dad *and* my best friend."

"I wish I deserved to be called that." I wiped away a stream of tears.

"You're still my best friend. This doesn't change that." She leaned forward. "I need to see the Taylor Abernathy that used to put every privileged asshole at Carson Cove High in their place—where's she at? Come on..."

"Give her a few minutes—she's still processing it." Anna's voice echoed from the doorway, and I had no idea how long she had been standing there. "Taylor thought you would be angrier at her than Alexis—I was about fifty-fifty on it myself."

"Anna?" Victoria jumped up and walked over to hug my little sister. "My god, you're almost grown!"

"It's only been a couple of years, jeez." Anna let Victoria hug her, but then squirmed out of her grasp. "I've got someone I want you to meet."

"Huh?" I looked up in confusion—and then saw someone walk up behind her that I already knew—by name at least.

"This is Bolt." She smiled and looked at him. "Bolt, the girl that's crying is my sister, Taylor. This is her—I guess—*still*, best friend, Victoria."

"Pleasure to meet you both." He had a calm, soothing voice—and gave us a polite nod. "My name is Gavin Bolton."

"Hi..." I wiped away what was left of my tears and shook his hand. "I saw you at the scrimmage game with Carson Cove University—you looked like a star out there."

"He *is* a star." Anna grinned. "Wait—you were at the game? You already knew..."

"It wasn't my place." I held up my hands and turned to Bolt. "I'm sorry we had to officially meet under these circumstances…"

"That's actually why he's here." Anna grabbed Bolt's hand and led him into the living room.

"I don't understand…" Victoria looked at me and my face obviously had the same confused stare.

"Well, in addition to being the star running back at Carson Cove High—we're going to state, by the way." Anna nudged her boyfriend, who nodded in agreement. "He's also quite proficient with a laptop."

"My brother showed me a few things." Bolt nodded. "Bad things, mostly—like how to hack into a database."

"I'm lost." Victoria looked at Bolt. "What are we hacking exactly?"

"Devereaux Properties." Anna sat down next to Bolt as he pulled out his laptop. "I've been thinking about what Taylor told me—and if Alexis Devereaux has this much power, I doubt it's because of her generosity. People hate her—like, *everyone* hates her."

"That's true…" Victoria raised an eyebrow. "I've never met anyone that was happy to see her. When I was dating her son, she was always screaming at someone on the phone or yelling at them in her office—except her brother. He seemed to be the only person in the world she could tolerate."

"Blackmail…" I nodded. "How else could she get my mother fired and have me set up for plagiarism at school—she's got dirt on people."

"There's plenty of it in Carson Cove." Victoria poured a glass of wine and sat down. "Enough to fill the Grand Canyon twice…"

"But if she has dirt on people, I doubt it's going to be just sitting on a server at Devereaux Properties." I shook my head back and forth.

"Where else would she keep it?" Anna looked up at me. "Her cell phone? Her personal computer? That's too dangerous—especially if it's the kind of stuff that can coerce people into doing things, they don't want to do…"

"It's worth a shot." Victoria shrugged. "She's obviously got something on my dad, and if we can figure out what that is, we might be able to put a stop to this wedding before you have to try on a dress…"

"That—would be nice." I nodded.

Bolt was a good hacker—by my standards at least. He was able to get into the Devereaux Properties database, and access a lot of confidential stuff, but none of it appeared to be helpful. We found a lot of purchase orders, deals that Sawyer King made when he was still married to Alexis, and it was clear that company was doing better than we had heard. In fact, it was quite profitable. That didn't really make sense to me. Alexis and her brother were co-owners of Devereaux Properties, so half of everything should have belonged to her.

Bolt kept digging until it started getting late—late enough for my mother to get home and wonder why there was a party at her house. Luckily, she didn't ask many questions after she said hello to Victoria and met Bolt for the first time. I didn't want to just give up, but it didn't seem like we were getting anywhere. We were just going in circles.

"I thought she was looking for a rich husband to marry…" I shook my head back and forth. "It looks like she's—loaded."

"My dad always said her father squandered the Devereaux fortune, and her brother's gambling problem is no secret, so— it made sense to me too." Victoria nodded. "What the hell is she after?"

"I'm sorry…" Bolt sighed. "It doesn't look like there's anything useful here."

"There has to be something we're missing," Anna grunted in frustration.

"I'll keep looking, but if I don't get home soon, my parents might send a search party for me." Bolt closed his laptop. "Or Coach Boyd—and I'd rather have the cops after me than him."

"I understand that," Victoria chuckled. "Okay, I think we need to call it a night. I'll approach things cautiously with my dad and see if I can figure out what the hell Alexis is up to—maybe I'll have better luck at Benson Estate."

We said our goodbyes, and I hugged Victoria one last time before she left. I felt better with my secret out in the open with her, but I still didn't feel good about the situation as a whole. Victoria was still my friend, but we had no idea how to take Alexis down—or stop the wedding. I was going to have to play Maid of Honor—and stand next to Alexis while she married the man that could have been mine. Our relationship never got to the point of talking about rings or dresses and it never would. It hurt even worse knowing that Victoria would have approached our relationship with maturity instead of disdain.

I should have cherished the time we had instead of fighting my feelings—I'd give anything to have that chance now...

Chapter Twenty-Two

BRYANT

"*D*on't..." I looked up at Victoria as she stormed into the living room. "You should be at school."

I knew she was coming in guns blazing as soon as I realized she was in Carson Cove...

"Do you really think I'm going to stay at school when my dad is about to make the biggest mistake of his life." She narrowed her eyes. "We need to talk about this."

"We talked on the phone. I told you—I'm marrying Alexis. That's the end of the discussion," I sighed. "It's my life. I get to choose who I want to be with—not you."

"Then tell me this." She took a step forward. "Would you rather be with Alexis—or *Taylor*."

"Taylor?" My mouth fell open in shock.

"I know everything, dad. So why don't we cut through the bullshit and talk about what's really going on here." She sat down across from me. "What does Alexis have on you?"

My youngest daughter had obviously made a stop on her way to Benson Estate—and found out the truth from Taylor. If she knew that, then there was no reason to hide the rest of it from her. She knew Shaina was in rehab, but she didn't know about the video, so I showed it to her. Alexis had promised to delete it after we said our vows, but she sent me a link in case I wanted to torture myself with a reminder of why we were headed to the altar. Victoria watched enough of the video to see why it was so bad before she finally shut it off.

"That video would ruin your sister's life," I sighed. "I don't know what she's going to do when she gets out of rehab, but I don't want it following her around. Alexis said she would send it to every potential employer, every school that she applies to—anyone that might give her another chance."

"Who filmed it?" Victoria raised an eyebrow.

"I don't know." I shrugged. "Based on the angle, it looks like some sort of security camera or something—but I didn't really see one in her apartment when I cleared it out…"

"Okay, then how did Alexis get her hands on it?" Victoria leaned forward. "Shaina was on the other side of the country…"

"Again, I don't know." I threw my hands up and sighed. "That doesn't really matter, does it? She has it—and that's enough. I can't let her ruin Shaina's life."

"You'll just let her ruin *your* life instead?" Victoria scoffed. "How is *that* fair?"

"What's fair about any of this?" I exhaled sharply and started to stand. "It's just money, Victoria. If Alexis wants it that bad, she can fucking have it. Welcome home. I'm going to bed."

"What about Taylor?" Victoria stood to her feet. "She still cares about you…"

"Taylor ended things—not me." I shook my head back and forth.

"Do you know why?" Victoria walked over and put her hand on my arm.

"No," I sighed and turned to face her. "The relationship

was tough from the beginning. She was worried that you would flip out if you knew—obviously you didn't."

"You need to sit back down, dad—because you need to know *exactly* what kind of woman you're about to marry." Victoria motioned to my chair. "Alexis went after Taylor too…"

"She did what!?" I felt my blood starting to boil.

The things Victoria told me were horrifying. If Alexis had been standing in front of me, I would have struggled not to snap her damn neck. If the bitch wanted to go after me—that was fine—but Taylor was innocent. She didn't do a damn thing wrong except fall for me as hard as I fell for her—she basically got turned into cannon fodder for Alexis' venomous agenda. I don't know what I would have been able to do if Taylor had been honest with me. I could have confronted Alexis, but it would have been impossible for me to take action if she had the video of Shaina. One thing was for damn sure—Alexis had to pay for what she had done. I just had no fucking idea how I was going to make that happen.

"Can you email me that link?" Victoria motioned to my tablet after I had finally stopped seething over where she told me.

"Why?" I tilted my head inquisitively.

"I know someone that might be able to help." She shrugged. "At this point, anything is worth trying."

I sent Victoria the link and went to bed. There was no way I was going to sleep, but I just wanted to be alone in the darkness. I couldn't believe Alexis had went after Taylor. Maybe I should have been suspicious—Alexis did show up right after Taylor ended our relationship, but I assumed it was speculation based on the fact that we hadn't been seen out since the auction. My world was no longer crashing around me—it was just shattered into pieces. I had a daughter in rehab, a daughter that had apparently decided to blow off school to come home and try to talk to some sense into me—and Dylan hadn't spoken to me since I told him I was marrying Alexis. I assumed he wasn't coming to the wedding—not that I really blamed him. I didn't expect anyone I cared about to be in attendance when I said my vows to the venomous bitch.

She's going to have to drag me to the altar kicking and screaming now that I know what she did to Taylor. Our relationship never should have ended—if I had known why it did, then I would have fought harder before I gave up…

Several days later

"Yes, you can take down the Picasso. I don't like that one. Put it in storage—actually, put it up for auction…" Alexis' voice echoed from the living room, and I immediately started walking towards her.

"Alexis, what the hell are you doing here." I walked in to find her with two guys that I didn't recognize.

"Just a little redecorating… I hired a moving company to help." She looked around the living room. "Yes, get rid of that one too—who is that anyway? Monet? I'll buy a couple of Rembrandts to add some atmosphere to the room…"

"Stop!" I walked over and grabbed the guy's arm when he reached for the Picasso. "Alexis, we aren't married—yet. You don't get to storm in here and start moving my shit around."

"Fine…" She rolled her eyes. "I'll wait until the paperwork is signed."

"You two can go." I growled at the guys from the moving company, and they quickly made their exit.

"You can go too." She waved at me as if she was shooing a dog from the room.

"No, I think *you* should be the one to go." I narrowed my eyes.

"Don't be silly." She laughed and shook her head. "I need the room. They're bringing my wedding dress by so I can try it on—you know what they say about seeing the bride in her dress before the big day!"

"You couldn't try on your dress at Devereaux Estate?" I tilted my head to the side.

"No, of course not. We're getting married here—I want to see how it looks in the light. That's why I wanted the paintings changed—they're depressing." She gave me a bewildered shake of her head.

"The paintings stay..." I growled at her. "Fuck, whatever—try on your damn wedding dress." I turned and walked towards the library—I definitely needed a drink.

Victoria had been trying to get dirt on Alexis, but she was running into a wall—just like I had when I tried to figure her out. The only thing I had managed to accomplish was meeting with Addison Regan—a high powered attorney that lived in the city. She helped me set up a trust in Victoria's name, and I used it to transfer ownership of the purchase agreement for Alcott Inc. The trust would buy the company when the deal was finalized, and it would be outside of Alexis' grasp. I couldn't do that with Benson Enterprises—a transfer of ownership would ruin the company—if there was anything left of it after I married Alexis.

I won't stop fighting until I'm forced to say my fucking vows—there has to be a way to put that venomous bitch in her place.

Several of my employee had already quit, others were threatening to do the same, and a number of clients pulled their investments. I couldn't blame them. In their eyes, I was either an idiot for marrying Alexis Devereaux or an asshole that supported her business tactics. Either option made them terrified to be associated with me. I hated going to work every day and looking the same people in the eyes that believed me when I said I would never be involved with someone like Alexis. I guess *liar* could be added to the list of awful things people were saying about me—I certainly felt like one.

"Yes, she needs to try on her dress too, but do it in the other room." Alexis' infuriating voice made me want to claw my eardrums out—I couldn't even escape it when I was in the library.

"Right this way, ma'am. I believe we've picked out the perfect dress for you to stand by her side..." Another voice—but what they said piqued my interest.

Stand by her side? Is Taylor here?

I walked down the hallway—carefully. I didn't want Alexis to hear me. I caught a glimpse of the tailor that she hired to do alterations on her wedding dress, so I ducked out of sight—then I saw Taylor. She looked like a damn angel—a sight for sore eyes that had been aching to see her beautiful face. The tailor didn't seem very concerned with Taylor or the dress she needed to try on—he led her to one of the other rooms and returned to Alexis. I darted down the hallway, made sure I wasn't spotted, and slipped into the room where Taylor was. I immediately closed the door and locked it.

"Huh?" Taylor spun around. "Bryant! Alexis said you weren't going to be here..."

"She lied." I walked towards Taylor and tried to hug her, but she pushed me away.

"We—we shouldn't do that." She shook her head rapidly.

"I don't give a damn about what we should or shouldn't do." I pulled her close and stared into her eyes. "I'm going to kiss you—and if you don't want me to, you damn sure better scream..."

"I..." There was no scream—just the hint of a smile.

I kissed Taylor and there was only a second of hesitation before she started kissing me back. Our lips seared together as I started to ravage her mouth. My hands moved along her curves and she dug her nails into my back. I kissed her until my head was spinning and my cock was throbbing my pants, but I finally forced myself to pull away.

"I'm going to find a way for us to be together. I don't know how—not yet—but just trust me," I exhaled sharply as my lips separated from hers. "Victoria told me what Alexis did to you and why you ended our relationship…"

"I was already torn up about it. I didn't like the fact that we were hiding it from Victoria—or anyone else." Taylor looked down and sighed.

"Once this is over, we're not going to hide a damn thing." I pressed my lips to her forehead.

"She has the video…" Taylor grimaced. "You have to marry her—you can't let that get out and ruin Shaina's life."

"I know…" I sighed.

"Is everything okay in there?" The tailor knocked on the door.

"Yes—just—trying on the dress," Taylor answered him, and I tried not to make a sound.

"Alright, I'll be back to check on you soon. Mrs. Devereaux is having some problems with hers…" His voice trailed off, and he walked away.

"You should do what you said." I raised an eyebrow and smiled. "Try on the dress… I don't think it's bad luck for the groom to see the Maid of Honor in her dress before the wedding."

"You just want to see me try to squirm into it." She narrowed her eyes—but a hint of a smile formed on the edge of her lips. "Alexis bought one that is one size too small—and told me to go on a *diet* so I can fit into it."

"That fucking bitch…" I shook my head.

"It doesn't matter…" Taylor walked over to the dress. "If I

pop out of the dress at the wedding, I guess nobody will be staring at the bride."

"I'm not going to be looking at the bride anyway." I walked up behind Taylor and pressed my lips to her neck. "My eyes will be on the prettiest girl in the room."

"This isn't fair…" She shook her head back and forth.

"No, it isn't." I moved my lips to her ear. "But we've got a few minutes—why waste them?"

I started kissing Taylor's ear—moved then down to her neck—and then she turned around to kiss me. My hands pulled at her clothes as she pulled at mine. I honestly didn't care if Alexis found us together—I should have, considering what she could do to both of us, but the heat of the moment consumed me. It wasn't like I was ever going to consummate my tainted marriage to Alexis. I lifted Taylor up onto the desk, pushed her legs apart, and stripped her panties off as she unbuckled my belt. I lifted up as soon as my cock was free and found her wetness—then I started to push my way inside her.

"I've missed this so fucking much," I exhaled sharply into her ear.

"We—oh god—we have to be quick." Taylor slid closer and moved her hips until I was buried inside her pussy.

I began to thrust—slowly—and as quietly as possible. My lips found hers, and I crushed them beneath mine. We kissed as the passion consumed our soul. It wasn't going to take long—for either of us. Our bodies were practically screaming for the contact we both craved. The desk wasn't the most sturdy one in the house—the room wasn't used often. I had to slow down every time the momentum got good, but it felt amazing, none-theless. I devoured Taylor's lips—savored every second of our kiss—and hoped it wouldn't be the last time I tasted her bliss.

"Don't stop…" She pulled her lips away and gasped. "I'm gonna come!"

"Oh fuck, me too…" I tightened my grip on her and gave her a few thrusts that were harder than the others.

Taylor's pussy began to spasm and made my balls twitch. I didn't try to restrain myself or hold back. I just kept thrusting as the cum surged through my shafted and erupted into her climax. I tried to send a few hard thrusts into her g-spot to make the orgasm peak for a few more seconds before it started to fade, and I slowed my thrusts as we came down from our high. I didn't want to let her go, but the release brought clarity, and I realized just how much our lust could cost us. I slowly pulled out and kissed her one last time before pulling away.

"I have to put on my dress…" She reached for her panties.

I quickly dressed as she squirmed into her dress—it was definitely one size too small, and Taylor's curves were perfect—she didn't need to lose a single pound. Alexis was just being a total bitch. I helped her get the dress on, got dressed, and then there was a knock at the door. I scrambled over to the closet and hid in it while she let the tailor in. He checked her a few times, seemed satisfied with the result, and then went back to tend to the bride.

"That was close…" I chuckled under my breath after he was gone.

"Yeah, you need to get out of here." Taylor leaned against me. "Thank you—I needed that."

"Don't give up hope." I kissed her forehead. "We're going to find a way to get through this."

This moment just added more fuel to my fire. Taylor and I can be together once I put an end to this fucking charade.

Two weeks later

J was ready to bang my head against the wall. I felt like I was being pulled in every direction at the same time. Benson Enterprises was struggling—to the point that we could actually be in real trouble if another big investor pulled out. Shaina was asking to see me, so I needed to make a trip to the city. I hadn't been able to see Taylor since the moment we stole while she was at my house—and I was dying inside every day that passed without being able to hold her in my arms. The wedding was approaching fast. We only had two weeks until the date that Alexis chose to for us lie our way through our vows. Victoria had decided to remain in Carson Cove, but thankfully her university was allowing her to handle her classes online until she could return.

"Cassie, please cancel my meetings for tomorrow." I sighed and shook my head. "I'm going to be out of the office."

"More wedding plans?" She gave me a dry smile.

"No…" I aimlessly tapped her desk with my fingers. "I have to take a trip to the city."

"Great, I'll take care of it." She looked up at me. "Oh, I wanted you to know that I'm putting in my two weeks notice today—you should probably start interviewing secretaries."

"What?" I blinked in confusion. "Why?"

"You know why, Mr. Benson." She turned back towards her computer.

Fuck…

Cassie was another casualty of my bastardized union with the venomous bitch. I couldn't blame her. There were so many empty seats on the floor already—why should my secretary stick around? I couldn't tell her the truth. I couldn't tell anyone the truth. I was living a lie every time I woke up and half the shit I said when I opened my mouth was spin doctoring. The only way I was able to lay my head down at night was because I knew it was for a good reason. If my life fell apart, so be it—I had taken care of the stuff that truly mattered. My kids had trust funds that were untouchable. Alcott Inc. was protected. Benson Enterprises couldn't be saved, but it wasn't like any of my kids wanted to work there—by the time I was ready to retire, it would go to someone else unless they changed their mind.

"Mr. Benson." Cassie turned towards me. "Your bride has arrived."

Fuck...

"What do you need, my dear?" I created the kindest version of a sarcastic tone I could muster—because it had to look somewhat normal in public.

"Let's talk in your office." She motioned towards it.

"Fine..." I walked into my office and waited until the door was closed. "What the fuck do you want!?"

"I've been thinking, darling..." She smiled and tilted her head. "After we're married, I want to be more involved in our family endeavors—I'd like for you to appoint me CEO of Alcott Inc."

"The fuck?" I tilted my head. "Don't you have your hands full with Devereaux Properties—I mean, when you do some-things besides torment people."

"Aidan can handle that." She waved off my concern. "Alcott Inc. will be a much better fit for me."

"Well that's not happening. I made an agreement with Jon to let him stay on as CEO after I bought the company." I narrowed my eyes and growled.

"I'll have my lawyer look into that." She turned towards the door. "See you soon—only two weeks until the big day."

Don't fucking remind me.

I headed to my car as soon as I was finished at the office. I wasn't in the mood to go home, because Alexis kept randomly stopping in to see me—or offer suggestions on the future decor. I wanted to see Taylor, and she wanted to see me, but we agreed that we should keep a low profile until we figured out what the fuck we were going to do. I decided to just stay in the city for the evening—Sarah had agreed to meet me for breakfast, and then we were going to see Shaina together. I hoped she was still doing well. She hadn't checked herself out of rehab, so I assumed things were moving in a positive direction.

One thing in my life is—I might as well be happy about it.

Chapter Twenty-Three

TAYLOR

"*D*amn it…" I stared at my phone. "Bryant's in the city and won't be back until tomorrow."

"We need him." Bolt looked up at me. "I'm almost there—I just need access to her phone."

"Are you sure about this?" Victoria leaned forward. "If we steal her phone and this doesn't get us what we want, then she's going to know we're up to something—she'll lock everything down."

"He's sure." Anna nodded. "That link you sent—it goes to a cloud."

"I've been trying to crack it for two weeks now," Bolt sighed. "I called my brother, and he said there's a way, but you need a device that's connected to it—we won't be able to unlock her phone since it's bound to her fingerprint, but he sent me a program that can get around the security."

"Maybe I can steal it…" Victoria shrugged. "Or—Taylor?"

"Me?" I blinked in surprise.

"You're her Maid of Honor." Victoria grinned. "That should make her open the door for you."

"That could work…" I nodded. "Fuck, if we get caught, she's going to ruin us all."

"I've got a plan." Anna pulled out a piece of paper and a pen. "This is *going* to work."

A few hours later

I played on Alexis' narcissism to get her to agree to meet me. Outside of my tryst with Bryant when we tried on four dresses, I had held up my end of the bargain as her Maid of Honor—and the one thing we hadn't figured out was the bachelorette party. She didn't deserve one, but she wanted all of the boxes checked—that was on the list. I had Victoria help me with an agenda, and since the wedding was two weeks away, Alexis said I could stop by Benson Estate and go over it with her. Bryant wasn't there—she shouldn't have been—but I didn't think it was my place to tell her that. Victoria had been avoiding the place like the plague and rented a room at on local bed and breakfast just to avoid having to see her stepmother-to-be.

"Taylor! Welcome…" Alexis flashed me a plastic smile and stepped to the side so I could enter.

"Hey…" I walked in.

"You have an agenda for my party? Come, let's review it." She motioned for me to follow her. "Honestly, I thought you were going to forget…"

"I told you I would do everything I'm supposed as Maid of Honor," I sighed as I followed her into the living room.

"Yes, well." Her smile faded as she sat down. "If you don't do what you're supposed to do, then I would be forced to call my friend Dean Richart—and neither of us wants this to get ugly, do we?"

"No." I tensed up immediately.

"Tell me, since it's just us girls..." She leaned forward. "How is he—in bed?"

"I'm sorry—what?" My head snapped back.

"I just want to know if I'm going to be *satisfied*." She flashed an evil grin. "I plan to ride that big, hard cock of his every single night once we're married."

Stay calm. Stay calm. Just stay calm.

"You'll be satisfied..." I looked down at the floor. "Can we talk about the party now?"

"Yeah, we'll get to that. I know he's getting a bit older now... Should I go ahead and get him a prescription for Viagra?" She tilted her head to the side. "Maybe I'll do that anyway—just in case."

Oh my god, she's such a miserable cunt.

"I'm sure you won't need it," I sighed. "The party?"

"Fine, let me see what you put together." She extended her hand and snapped her fingers at me like I was a dog.

Okay Victoria—here's your cue.

"Dad, are you here?" The front door opened, and Victoria walked in a few seconds after I hit the button on my phone to let her know it was time.

"Victoria?" Alexis put the agenda down on the table and looked up. "What are you doing here? Your father is in the city —visiting your sister."

"Shit, really?" Victoria pretended to be surprised. "Oh— *she's* here."

"I can go." I started gathering my things.

"Nonsense, we're talking wedding stuff." Alexis waved off my suggestion.

"It's—*fine*..." Victoria gave me the angriest glare she could muster. "I just need to grab some stuff out of my room."

Alexis had no idea that Victoria and I survived the bombshell about my relationship with her father. We figured it was best that she thought we hated each other to make it easier to work together on our real agenda. Victoria had done her best to be civil to Alexis in order to stay on her good side—but she knew she would eventually crack if she had to stay at Benson Estate. That, of course, made it seem like Bryant's relationship with his daughter was strained—and provided the perfect cover for why she would show up when he was out of town. Alexis reached for the agenda after Victoria walked off—and a second later there was a loud crash.

"Oh shit!" Victoria squealed.

"What the hell?" Alexis stood up. "I'll be right back."

Bryant fought Alexis' attempt to redecorate Benson Estate at every turn, but a few things had made their way there—like the ashes of Alexis' father. It was morbid, wrong, and so awful, but it was the best way to get a reaction out of the venomous bitch. Needless to say, when she turned the corner and saw the ceramic urn shattered and her father's ashes strewn all over the floor, she went ballistic. That was *my* cue. I grabbed Alexis' phone, swapped it out with the decoy we bought, and gathered my things. Alexis was screaming at Victoria and wailing when I made it to the door of the living room. She looked almost human in that moment, but I didn't care—she had drained whatever compassion I might have had for her humanity out of me long before our plan was made.

"You are a wretched little bitch; I swear to god!" Alexis pushed Victoria.

"I'm sorry! I'm so sorry! I didn't mean to!" Victoria faked her way to the verge of crocodile tears.

"I should just go. We'll discuss this later…" I made a quick dash for the door.

Bolt was waiting in the car—and a few seconds after I escaped from Benson Estate, Alexis' phone was in his hand. He plugged it into his laptop and started typing as I drove. That was it—our only play. If we got into Alexis' phone, then it was our best shot of bringing her down. If we failed, and the cloud didn't have what we were looking for—then it was over. Her retribution would be swift—there was a chance I would lose everything—but I didn't care anymore. If there was a chance that I could end Alexis' engagement with Bryant and bring the bitch to her knees, then I had to take it.

"I'm in!" Bolt practically jumped up and down in his seat.

"Oh my god…" Anna stared at the screen.

"What?" I looked over my shoulder.

"Pull over, Taylor. Pull over now!" Anna motioned to me.

We didn't just find what we were looking for—we hit the fucking jackpot. There were so many files—so much blackmail material—we could have brought down half of the families in Carson Cove. Every time we clicked one of them, we found something that made us either shake our head in disbelief or want to throw up. Bolt moved all of the files into his cloud, cleared Alexis' out, and wiped the backups.

"It's over…" Anna looked up at me. "She's finished."

"Are you sure she can't get the files back?" I couldn't help but feel worried.

"Her cloud is backed up, but that's it—there are no file transfers to other sources. All I see on the logs are transfers in. I've been through everything else." He nodded.

"Yeah, but where are those transfers coming from?" I tilted my head in concern.

"From her phone." He turned it towards me. "Emails mostly—but I'm going to wipe all of those and kill this phone to be safe."

"Wait…" I held up my hand. "If the transfers came from emails, it will probably implicate the people who were helping her. Can we back those up too?"

"Uh…" He narrowed his eyes. "It'll take a while—if she realizes we've got her phone, she could log in from another location and save some of them."

"Okay, forget it. Just wipe them all out." I nodded. "Wait, can you find the one with Shaina Benson?"

"Yeah, it's from a guy—at a security company I think?" He nodded.

"Forward that one to me." I turned back towards the steering wheel. "Wipe out the rest of them."

Bolt worked his magic, and I drove back to my house. It was another hour before Victoria showed up, and she practically screamed for joy when she found out that our mission was successful. I knew it was only a matter of time before Alexis figured out what we had done—and none of us were going to sleep easy—if we even slept at all. We had a lot of stuff to look through and try to figure out what we could undo—what we needed to send to the authorities—and we had to let Bryant know that he didn't have to marry the venomous bitch.

"Click that one." I pointed to a file. "That's the dean at Carson Cove University."

"Oh!" Bolt's eyes opened wide when the video started. "Yeah, I'm not watching this."

"He—likes to be dominated." I squinted and grimaced. "And that's definitely not his wife."

"What's that one? Isn't that mom's boss?" Anna pointed at the screen.

"Damn—Anna, you don't need to be watching *any* of this." I put my hand over her eyes when I saw my mom's boss climb into bed with another man—obviously there were a number of wives in Carson Cove that had no idea who they married.

"That's my sister…" Victoria exhaled sharply. "Can you just get rid of that one?"

"Yeah, of course." Bolt nodded and hit a button. "There—it's gone from my cloud now."

"The link doesn't work!" Victoria smiled when she tried the one that was supposed to lead her to the video.

"I have the name of the guy who sold it to her." I picked up my phone. "I'll forward it to you."

"Perfect." She smiled. "I'm sure my sister isn't the only one he has footage of—and the cops are going to love that."

"Oh man…" Bolt gulped—like, literally gulped. "You need to see this."

"What is it?" I leaned forward.

"This is—her file on Sawyer King." He raised an eyebrow.

"She should have plenty of dirt on him. They were married…" Victoria shrugged.

"No, you *really* need to look at this." He put the laptop on the table and started clicking.

Holy shit…

Chapter Twenty-Four

BRYANT

The next morning

I slept like a rock. The hotel room gave me a different perspective—or maybe the change of scenery just allowed me to feel like I wasn't stuck in the midst of chaos. I'm sure the whiskey I drank at the hotel bar had something to do with it too. Either way, I slept until the sun was up, and woke up feeling refreshed when I should have had a hangover. I immediately went over to start a pot of coffee—the hotel room didn't have anything I liked, but I just needed caffeine, so the cheap stuff would have to do. I reached for my phone, unplugged it from the charger, and then my eyes nearly bulged out of my head.

What the fuck? Did World War 3 start while I was asleep!?

I had missed calls and text messages from Taylor, Victoria, Sarah, numbers I didn't recognize, and I didn't even know how to start sorting through them all. It didn't take much sorting to figure out that they had a common theme. The ones from Taylor and Sarah were directing me to call Victoria. The ones from the unknown numbers were rants—and they were from Alexis. The ones from Victoria just said that I needed to call her. I quickly flipped over to dial her number—and I was fairly terrified to make the call.

"Victoria, what's going on? I'm sorry, I was asleep…" I exhaled into the phone.

"Dad! Oh my god. We got her!" Victoria's tone was hurried and excited.

"What? Alexis? How?" I blinked away the last bit of fog, because that news woke me right the hell up.

Victoria explained what they had done—and I would have scolded her for behaving so recklessly if it hadn't yielded results. I didn't understand half of what she was saying—or who the Bolt person was that she kept referencing other than the fact that he was dating Taylor's sister. She started rambling so fast that it was hard to follow what she was saying—it sounded like excited exhaustion—but the important part was crystal clear. I didn't have to marry Alexis. The wedding was off—because she was headed straight to prison when the cops found her.

"Dad just turn on the news. Right now—the story is on Carson Cove AM." She sounded like she was about to explode with joy.

I grabbed the remote and turned on television. It took me a couple of minutes to find Carson Cove's morning show in the city, but I found a station that was broadcasting it. The anchor was talking about a file that had been emailed to the station—a file that implicated the Devereaux family in several serious crimes. I tried to listen to the story and put Victoria on speakerphone since she was still frantically talking about what they had done.

"Wait a minute…" I tilted my head as I stared at the screen. "Sawyer King doesn't exist!?"

"No!" Victoria practically shouted into the phone. "He was just some actor they hired! The Devereaux family was behind everything!"

"Holy shit…" I shook my head in disbelief. "Wait—if they were behind it…"

"They were coming after Benson Enterprises!" Victoria finished my train of thought. "That's why she wanted to marry you—and that wasn't all she was after."

"Alcott Inc…" I nodded. "Of course."

"Yeah…" The excitement faded from Victoria's voice. "She had a lot of dirt on Mary Alcott—sadly, I think divorce was the right choice, but it was ultimately orchestrated by Alexis. She was planning to buy the company when it went on the open market…"

"Alexis and her brother ruined so many lives." I shook my head back and forth. "And for what? Money?"

"It *is* the root of all evil," Victoria sighed.

I watched the rest of the story with Victoria on speaker phone, and then I had to wrap up the call. I still had plans to meet with Sarah, and then we had to go see Shaina. I took a shower, got dressed, and when I got to the car, I called Taylor. We made plans to get together as soon as I got back to Carson Cove. I had to catch Sarah up over breakfast. She knew *something* was going on because Victoria called her looking for me—but she was fairly surprised when I told her the full story.

Shaina was very happy to see us, and she had asked me to come because she wanted to apologize for everything in person. I didn't need her apology—I forgave her as soon as I saw she was safe in the hospital—but it seemed to be important to her recovery. She had decided that she was going to stay in rehab for a little longer than originally planned, and then she planned to return to Carson Cove. I told her that she would always have a spot at Benson Enterprises if she wanted to work there—what was left of it at least. It was going to take a long time to restore it to its former glory, but I hoped things would move in that direction once people realized the truth about Alexis Devereaux.

My employees and clients put their trust in me. I let them down. Hopefully they'll understand why I had to do it when they realize what I was up against.

Later that day

I drove back to Carson Cove, and Taylor said she would be waiting on me at my house. I was anxious to see her, but I had a press conference to handle first. I had several calls from reporters who were wanting an interview, but I needed to make sure everyone heard what I had to say. The best way to do that was just stand in front of everyone and admit the truth. It might have bothered me more if I wasn't so happy to be rid of Alexis. I decided to hold it at Benson Enterprises, because the people there needed to hear it most of all. My lawyer met me in the lobby, we reviewed a few notes, and then I walked to the podium where I saw more reporters than I had ever seen in my life. It wasn't just the local reporters—there were a few national ones there as well.

Okay, this may be more difficult than I expected—fuck it.

"Good morning everyone. For those of you who don't know me, my name is Bryant Benson." I looked around the room.

"Mr. Benson!" A reporter in the front row raised his hand. "Do you have any comments about the Alexis Devereaux situation—you were engaged to be married, right?"

"I'm going to address all of that." I nodded. "I'll take questions after I'm done."

I started as close to the beginning as I could without saying Taylor's name. It wasn't fair for her to get pulled into the middle of a media frenzy. I told the reporters about the blackmail, without saying exactly what she had on me, and that it appeared Alexis' goal was to gain control of Benson Enterprises. I apologized to the people who worked for me—the investors that didn't trust me—and thanked those that stuck with me through the difficult time. I invited all of the people who had decided to leave Benson Enterprises to return—and promised them that I would make it up to them if they did. After that, I opened it up to questions.

"Mr. Benson, you said that Mrs. Devereaux was blackmailing you. Can you tell us what she had?" The reporter in the front row hit me with a hard question.

"Considering the fact that you agreed to marry her—I think people are going to wonder if she had something on you that could have put you in a cell beside her." A reporter in the back held her hand up as she spoke.

"Alexis Devereaux is an opportunist," I sighed. "All I can say is that she obtained access to something that would have ruined someone's life—and I wasn't going to let that happen— even if I had to marry her. I can assure you that I am not a criminal, and the situation has been addressed by the proper authorities."

That much was true. The police wouldn't have arrested Shaina without actual evidence and there was none in her apartment. My explanation seemed to quell the reporters, and they fired off a few more questions that I was able to easily answer. I didn't know if it would be enough to undo the damage that Alexis caused, but I would have to carry the weight of my part in it. I made a decision to protect my family, and I didn't regret that. I was just glad it was over. As soon as the press conference ended, I reconvened with my lawyer, we put together an official statement for the people that might not have seen the press conference, and I was finally able to head home. Taylor's car was in the driveway, and I couldn't even begin to contain my excitement.

"Welcome home…" Taylor walked out of the house as soon as I stepped out of my car—and the smile on her face was radiant.

"You don't know how long I've waited to see that smile." I ascended the stairs and nearly tackled Taylor as I pulled her into my arms for a kiss.

"I did a little redecorating while I was waiting…" She leaned back from our embrace after our lips finally parted.

"Really?" I raised an eyebrow and followed her inside.

"I think this is everything that Alexis changed." She motioned to a pile on the floor. "I don't know where the stuff you had there before went…"

"She had some movers put it in the west wing of the house. I'll take care of it later…" I put an arm around Taylor. "God, I just want to burn all of this shit."

"Why can't we?" Taylor grinned and looked up at me.

She was right, so that's exactly what we did. We carried everything that belonged to Alexis out of the house and set it on fire. It was rather cathartic to see all of the stuff Alexis brought to my house go up in flames—and get reduced to ash. I fought her changes in the beginning, but she was persistent— I didn't even realize she had moved so much stuff in—obviously she had used my trip to the city as an excuse to make some changes I previously stopped her making. We saved the art for Mr. Wellington. He could keep the profits for charity for all I cared. We watched until the fire burned out, and then we walked back inside—where we shared a long, passionate kiss before we went into the living room to talk. I didn't want to talk—I wanted to take her upstairs immediately—but there were a few things we needed to work through first.

"You know…" I looked up at the wall when we got into the living room. "I think instead of replacing the Monet, I want to put something else there."

"Oh?" Taylor raised an eyebrow. "What's that?"

"I'm thinking—a new artist." I nodded. "It looks like a good place for my first Taylor Abernathy."

"You've never even seen my work." She laughed and shook her head.

"Then I guess you better show it all to me—that way I can figure out which one I want to buy." I shrugged and chuckled under my breath.

"It's really over…" Taylor moved closer to me.

"Yes." I kissed her forehead. "Which means the two of us can pick up where we left off the last time we were in here…"

"I wish we could, but Victoria will be here soon." Taylor looked up at me. "She asked me to text her once you arrived—I can't put it off all night."

"Okay." I nodded. "I guess you're right—she probably does want to celebrate."

"You and I can celebrate later tonight…" Taylor put her hand on my thigh and teased me with a touch.

"Text Victoria—the faster we get that part of the evening over with, the faster we can have our own celebration." I kissed Taylor's neck and pressed my lips to her ear. "I love you."

"I love you too," she moaned and finally broke away from our embrace to pick up her cell phone.

Taylor and I made out for a few minutes, and then discussed a few things about our relationship while we waited on Victoria. She wanted to come clean with her mother, and I agreed that it was the right thing to do. I still needed to tell the rest of my family—I hoped they would react as well as Victoria had. Taylor was a part of my world regardless, and I wasn't going to let *anything* come between us again. Our relationship was nearly derailed before it could truly begin, but we had the rest of our lives to make up for it.

All that matters, is that she's in my arms now—and that's where she's going to stay.

Epilogue

Three months later

The police arrested Aidan Devereaux within a few days of the story breaking—the District Attorney just had to figure out which charges he deserved for his part in everything that happened in Carson Cove. Alexis tried to run —which wasn't that surprising. She hid out in the city with a friend for a few weeks, but she was finally arrested when she got into an argument with an employee at a coffee shop because her order wasn't right. Someone in the crowd recognized her, and it didn't take the police long to show up.

There was a mountain of evidence against her, and lives that had been destroyed by the Devereaux siblings, but she still managed to cut a deal with the District Attorney. Ten years in a white collar prison that was basically a resort wasn't nearly enough for everything she had done, but at least she was gone. The deal, of course, was to testify against her brother—which she turned into a performance that could have earned her an Emmy. If I didn't know how much of a venomous, manipulative bitch she was, I might have believed it myself. Aidan got forty years in a federal prison—with no possibility of parole. He would be an old man before he ever saw the light of day— if he lived that long.

"This is hardly justice…" Bryant sighed and shook his head as we watched the sentencing on the news.

"No, but she's gone." I shrugged. "A lot of people are sleeping easier in Carson Cove right now knowing that the blackmail she had against them is gone."

"Your sister's boyfriend deleted it all, right?" Bryant narrowed his eyes. "He seems like a good kid, but that kind of power can be tempting…"

"Yeah." I nodded. "I watched it myself. As soon as we decided what to send to the television station, the rest of it was wiped out—permanently."

"Good…" Bryant kissed my forehead. "Oh, I've got a surprise for you—we got distracted by the news story—come with me."

"A surprise?" I raised an eyebrow as he stood and helped me to my feet.

"Yep." Bryant led me down the hall—to a familiar room— one that we shared a moment of passion in during the midst of Alexis' tyranny.

"What is this?" I blinked in surprise as he opened the door.

"Since you're going to be spending a lot of time here, I thought you should have your own art studio." She walked into the room and turned back towards me. "It might be a little more comfortable than painting in your bedroom."

"Oh my god…" I smiled and hugged him. "This is —amazing!"

"That's not all." He hugged me, and then pulled away. "I've got one more surprise…"

Bryant presented me with a card—it was an invitation—to an art show at Wellington's. My eyes nearly bulged out of my head when I realized that my name was the featured attraction.

Bryant explained that a few of his friends had seen the painting in his living room—and demanded to know who the artist was. They were able to show enough interest for Mr. Wellington to come to him with a proposal for an art show—as long as I agreed not to sell anything until the next annual auction. Mr. Wellington was sure that people would be salivating to own one of them by then.

"I don't even know if I have enough paintings for an art show…" I stared at the invitation in disbelief.

"Then you better get started immediately." He motioned to the canvas. "You've got a few months until the show, and then you can figure out what you want to sell at the auction."

"What if they hate them?" I felt a lump rising up in my throat. "I gave you the best one…"

"They're amazing." He pulled me into his arms. "Just like you…"

Six months later

"*T*aylor, can you come into the living room for a minute?" My mother called out to me as I was walking towards the door.

"Yeah?" I stopped in my tracks and turned towards the door

"Don't go anywhere…" She stood up and walked through the door on the opposite side of the room.

She called me in here to—wait?

"Hey there…" A voice from behind startled me—a voice I knew as well as my own.

"Bryant?" I turned around and tried to hide the confusion on my face. "What are you doing here? I was just on my way to your place…"

"I wanted to do this here—well, after I talked to your mom, of course." He smiled.

"Do—what?" I tilted my head inquisitively.

Before I even realized what was happening, Bryant dropped down to one knee and pulled a square box out of his pocket. My head started spinning, and I barely even heard his proposal. He opened the box and revealed a beautiful diamond solitaire. I stumbled over my words as I tried to say—*anything*. Bryant went from smiling to slightly concerned as I mumbled my way towards the one word that mattered.

"I—yes!" I nodded quickly.

"I thought you were going to reject me there for a minute." A look of relief swept over his face as he slid the diamond on my ring finger and stood.

"I'm sorry!" I hugged him. "You caught me off guard!"

"It wouldn't be a surprise if you saw it coming." My mother walked into the room—followed by Anna—and someone else...

"Dad!?" I nearly fell over in shock.

"I couldn't propose without talking to your family." Bryant squeezed my hand. "I'm a bit old-fashioned, I suppose."

"How are you?" I pulled away from Bryant and hugged my father. "Wait—is this okay?"

I don't think my parents have been in the same room with each other since he left...

"We had a lot to discuss." My mother nodded. "But he's still your dad."

Both of my parents knew about Bryant. I came clean with my mother shortly after the ordeal with Alexis. She was surprised, but after we talked about it, she said she would support me. Bryant and I visited my dad in the city a few weeks later, and he was hesitant to accept the relationship, but he knew Bryant was a good man. Apparently, *something* had happened between that visit and Bryant's proposal, because they were both smiling—and demanding to see ring.

"Hold on, let me get a look at it first." Anna pulled my hand towards her and grinned. "Wow, it's beautiful!"

"Victoria helped me pick it out—she said her best friend deserved the best." Bryant chuckled. "Obviously, I agree with that…"

We were officially engaged, which meant that a wedding was in our future, and I had a lot of planning to do before graduation. Somewhere between finishing school and making plans for my wedding, I had to find time to paint. My art show was a resounding success—and I didn't think I was going to have enough paintings to meet the demand for my work—especially if Bryant kept snatching up the good ones.

"So, are you actually going to be able to take time off for the honeymoon?" I tilted my head inquisitively towards Bryant.

"Yes, I think Benson Enterprises can manage for a few days." He laughed and nodded.

"A few days…" I shook my head back and forth. "Could we try for a week?"

"I'll have to see if Cassie can fit something in…" He pulled me in for another hug. "I'm sure we can figure something out. Things are back to normal now, and most of my old employees have returned—they should be able to survive for a week without me."

I peeked at my engagement ring over Bryant's shoulder while he hugged me. I never imagined our relationship would ever make it that far when we were sneaking around, but things had worked out quite well for us after we got past the challenges. I was looking forward to my life with him—there was no doubt in my mind that we would be happy. We had even discussed adding to the Benson family down the road, and that was going to be on the horizon sooner than I realized.

Hopefully he still remembers how to change diapers…

Daddy's Best Friend: Sneak Peek

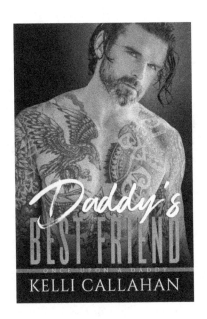

Chrissy

"Are you…" The man in front of me looked down at his sign,

which had my name written on it with a black marker. "Christina Banks?"

"Yes." I nodded and tilted my head slightly. "Are you—Mr. Foster?"

He doesn't look like the guy my mother described—but it's been a while I guess…

"No. My name is John." He shook his head back and forth. "I'm just here to pick you up. I'll take your bags."

"Thank you." I handed him the duffel bag that was hanging on my shoulder and took a step back so that he could pick up my luggage.

I didn't have much with me. I certainly didn't pack eighteen years of my life into a suitcase and a duffel bag. I brought the essentials, and the rest of my things were supposed to arrive in a few days. I still wasn't bringing everything that I owned from Chicago to Los Angeles, but I hoped I would have enough to make it through my first semester of college at the University of Southern California. It was my father's alma mater, and I had been planning to spend my college years there since I was a little girl—I just didn't expect to run into the complications that arose after I got a scholarship for everything except room and board.

"How far is it to Mr. Foster's house?" I followed John outside and waited as he loaded my things into the trunk of a black sedan parked by the curb.

"In this traffic?" He slammed the trunk and put his hands on his hips. "It'll take us about an hour to get there."

"Okay." I nodded and walked around to the side of the car.

John opened the back door and closed it once I was seated. The car was really nice. I had never been driven before—by an actual driver. My mother said that Mr. Foster was well off, which was why he was in a position to help, but she didn't tell me that he was rich enough to have his own driver. I hoped he was as nice as she said because I was still nervous about living with someone I didn't know. It was a temporary arrangement, and she vouched for him, but he was still a stranger to me. I knew him by name—and vaguely remembered him stopping by when I was younger—but I didn't really *know* him.

"So, have you been working for Mr. Foster very long?" I leaned forward and tried to make conversation once the car pulled onto the highway.

"A few years." John nodded. "He's a good boss."

"Cool…" I leaned back in my seat—I really couldn't think of anything else to ask him.

Mr. Foster—or Greyson, as my mother called him—was my father's best friend. I was really excited when I got accepted to USC, but when I realized that my scholarship wasn't going to cover anything outside of my educational expenses, I thought I was out of luck. My father left us with a little bit of money after he passed, but there was no way that my mother could afford to pay for me to live in California.

She saw how disappointed I was when I realized that my dream was about to fizzle out and decided to ask Mr. Foster for help. I hoped he would help me get an apartment and cover a couple of months of rent until I could get a job—instead, he offered to let me live with him while I was going to school. I didn't want to be a charity case, but it was an amazing offer—one that I couldn't really turn down. I still hoped that I would be able to get my own place after I got a job, but I was over-whelmed by his generosity.

"I don't think Mr. Foster is home from work yet, but your bedroom should be ready." John pulled the car up to a large iron gate and used a remote to open it.

"That's…" My eyes nearly bulged out of my head as I stared at the mansion ahead of us. "That's his *house*?"

"He's got a few." John chuckled. "But yes—this is where he lives."

I couldn't help being a little jealous when the car came to a stop in front of Mr. Foster's mansion. It was clear that being a sports agent in Los Angeles was a lot more lucrative than Chicago. My father barely left us with enough to get by—Mr. Foster was living in the lap of luxury. I followed John into the house, and he led me to a bedroom at the top of a large spiral staircase. I had to blink a couple of times to make sure I wasn't dreaming. It was certainly better than what I was used too. The room was nearly as big as the house I grew up in, and it appeared that I had my own bathroom—I was used to sharing a half-bath with my sister and fighting over the mirror in the morning was a daily battle.

"If you need anything, you can hit the red button on your telephone." John motioned to a phone that was sitting next to the bed.

"Who does that call?" I raised my eyebrows inquisitively.

"Mr. Foster has an assistant named Lauren who takes care of everything. If you need something, she'll handle it." He nodded quickly. "If you need to go somewhere, she'll call me."

"Oh wow, okay." I blinked in surprise.

John left me alone in my new bedroom, and I decided to start unpacking. The walk-in closet was enormous, and I certainly didn't have enough stuff to fill it. I could have stacked all of the boxes that were on the way to Los Angeles in the back corner of the closet and still had room to do cartwheels. There was a large dresser that looked more like a wardrobe. All of the socks and underwear I owned would fit in *one* of the drawers. I probably wouldn't have needed more than two to hold all of the socks and underwear I had *ever* owned. The bed was king sized and even bigger than the one in my mother's bedroom. I wondered if it was a California King. They were supposed to be bigger than regular ones—and I *was* in California.

I should take a few pictures and send them to my sister. Lorrie is going to be so freaking jealous.

I pulled out my phone, snapped a few panoramic shots, and then walked into the bathroom. There was a large whirlpool tub that reminded me of a Jacuzzi, and *two* shower heads. The sink was a large oval basin that I could have fit in if I curled up in a ball, and the mirror covered the entire wall behind it. There were also lights on the side of the mirror, which—unfortunately, made me realize I had a couple of blackheads that needed to be handled. I didn't even notice them when I was getting ready that morning. The mirror made the blackheads stand out so much that I dug into my purse and grabbed my makeup so I could add an extra layer to hide them until I had time to properly handle the problem.

Now what? I guess I could explore the rest of the house…

I walked downstairs and started looking around. The first room I came to appeared to be a library. There was a large oak desk in the middle of the room and more books than I thought anyone could read in one lifetime. I saw some pictures on the wall and walked over to get a better look. I had to assume the guy that appeared in all of them was Greyson Foster. He was —*hot*. My sister remembered him a lot better than I did, and she mentioned that he was attractive, but that was an understatement. He was standing next to a celebrity from movies or sports in almost every picture, and he looked like *he* was the star.

He knows a lot of famous people…

In the middle of all the celebrities was a picture of Mr. Foster with my father. Seeing my father's face was enough to make my eyes tear up. I was only five years old when he passed away. Most of the memories I had of him were stories that other people had told me. I was so young when he passed that I didn't have many of my own. My father was a little older than Mr. Foster, but not by much. My father just didn't take good care of himself—and he had a few vices, although most people didn't mention those when they talked about how great he was. I missed him, even though I didn't get a chance to really get to know him.

"You must be Christina." A voice startled me, and I turned around to see the man in all of the photographs standing in the doorway of the library.

Oh my god, is that a—British accent? My mother mentioned that he was a Rugby star in England before he became a sports agent…

"Hi! Mr. Foster!" I walked over and extended my hand. "Most people call me Chrissy."

"Chrissy…" He took my hand and shook it. "*Nobody* calls me Mr. Foster. Greyson—or *hey, you—yeah you* will work just fine."

Wow, every word he says sound like poetry—and he's so much hotter in real life…

"It's nice to meet you—again. I know I met you when I was younger, but I barely remember it." I looked up at him and for a second, I got lost in his mesmerizing brown eyes.

"You've definitely changed a little bit since then…" He narrowed his eyes. "I'm guessing you don't play with Barbie dolls anymore."

"No." I blushed and suppressed a grin. "Thank you so much for letting me stay here. I promise I won't stay any longer than I have to—a couple of months at most."

Hopefully I can afford my own place by then if I find a job.

"It's no trouble at all." A slight smile formed behind his neatly trimmed beard—it was a darker shade of brown than his eyes with a little bit of gray along his chin. "I have plenty of room and your father was like a brother to me. You can stay as long as you like."

If I stare at that amazing smile too long, I might never want to leave…

"I really appreciate it…" I nodded and forced myself to look away.

"Are you hungry? I assume you haven't eaten anything since Chicago?" He turned and started walking down the hallway.

"Now that you mention it…" I followed behind him.

Greyson walked into what appeared to be the living room. It had a fireplace and the biggest television I had ever seen. The couch was big enough to seat my extended family and looked like it was more comfortable than the *bed* I slept in at home. There were several photographs on the wall in the living room as well, but most of them appeared to be pictures of his family. It looked like Greyson had a couple of brothers that were younger but not quite as attractive as him—and a sister that was absolutely stunning. If the picture of his father was any indication, then Greyson was going be even hotter once he had a little more gray in his beard and a few streaks in his hair.

I've never really been attracted to an older man before, but Greyson is so freaking hot that I can't stop staring…

"Do you eat normal stuff, or should I ask my chef to start researching how to cook tofu?" He tilted his head inquisitively.

"I eat pretty much anything." I shrugged. "Except—like, anchovies on my pizza."

"Okay, good." He chuckled under his breath. "I don't like those either."

Greyson picked up the phone and hit the red button at the bottom. He asked his assistant to have some food delivered and even the word *cheeseburger* sounded sexy when he said it. I thought he was going to have something delivered, based on the conversation, but instead—a chef showed up and started preparing our meal. I wasn't sure if he just appeared on command like John or if it was some sort of special service rich people could order. A cheeseburger and fries in my world meant a trip to a fast food restaurant. I would have been happy with that, but Greyson didn't seem like the fast-food type.

I doubt he maintains that incredible physique on a diet of cheeseburgers and fries. If he does, then I need to know his secret.

"Let me give you the grand tour while our food is being prepared." Greyson walked towards the door and motioned for me to follow him.

"Sounds good." I nodded. "I only made it as far as the library—well, and my bedroom—which is awesome, by the way."

"Awesome enough for you to consider staying longer than a couple of months?" He looked over his shoulder at me.

"I just don't want to impose…" My words trailed off when he opened the door at the end of the hall, and I saw an enormous indoor pool. "Wow!"

"There's a pool and a jacuzzi in here." He waved his hand for me to follow. "A steam room over there…"

"This is incredible…" I stared in disbelief.

"The indoor pool is heated. The outdoor pool is not." He pointed to the window.

"Two—two swimming pools?" I walked over to the window and blinked in surprise.

I definitely didn't want to impose, but it was hard to imagine cramming myself into a small apartment when I had an offer to live with Greyson until I graduated from college. The rest of the house was just as amazing. There was an indoor gym complete with a basketball court, and the downstairs had a movie theater—like an actual movie theater with an IMAX screen and reclining chairs. He even had a small room next to it with a popcorn machine and a soda fountain. I wasn't sure what he *didn't* have. I wouldn't have been surprised if there was a freaking grocery store somewhere in his house.

"Alright, the food should be ready." He started walking back towards the kitchen area.

Greyson asked about my family once we sat down to eat—how my mother was doing and whether or not my sister's boyfriend had finally proposed. It seemed that he kept in contact with my mother regularly, even though she didn't mention him much. He told me a couple of stories about my father from when they were younger and worked together in Chicago. I had never heard much about that side of my father's life. It was painful for my mother to talk about him, so I didn't ask many questions. Most of what I knew about the man who passed away long before his time came from my sister, who was old enough to remember him better than I could.

"Something we need to discuss…" Greyson leaned back once he was done with his meal. "While you're staying here, whether it's for a few months or longer—I have a few rules."

Not surprising. I'd have rules too if this was my house.

"Of course." I nodded. "This is your house and I'm just a guest."

"I don't like having strangers here when I'm not home." He tilted his head slightly and smirked. "So, no sneaking boys in while I'm at work."

"Oh gosh." I blushed and chuckled under my breath. "I definitely won't do that."

I didn't have a boyfriend to sneak into my house when I was in high school, and I doubt that's going to change just because I'm in a different state.

"You're going to be in college, and I remember how that is, but you need to be home at a reasonable hour. If you decide to go out and have a drink or something, I won't judge you, but please don't drive. John will pick you up—anytime, wherever you are." He folded his arms across his chest. "Even if you're not living here."

"I appreciate that. That won't be an issue though. I don't drink—and I don't have a car…" I shrugged slightly.

"You're welcome to use any of mine if you want." He pointed towards the wall. "Except the Maserati. That's the one I drive."

"How many cars do you have?" I looked where he was pointing and saw a rack with at least a dozen sets of keys. "Oh wow!"

"If you use one of my cars, please stay off your cell phone —no texting and driving." He tilted his head slightly. "I mean that. Your mother will kill me if something happens to you when I'm supposed to be looking after you."

"Yeah, no problem." I nodded quickly. "Wait—looking after me?"

"Of course." He narrowed his eyes. "Don't get me wrong, I'm not your babysitter, but you're still a kid…"

Ouch…

"I mean…" I looked down at the table for a moment. "I'm eighteen. I think I can manage on my own…"

"Maybe, but you're still my responsibility while you are living here." He slid his chair back and started to stand.

"Are those all of the rules?" I looked up at him, feeling slightly offended that he thought I was just some kid he had to look after.

"The basics, yeah." He nodded. "Just stay out of trouble."

"I don't think that will be a problem." I looked away before he could see me roll my eyes.

"Good to hear. I'd hate to have to ground you or something." He chuckled and started walking towards the door.

Great, so this is basically like high school—except I live in a mansion and I get to drive a fancy car if I want…

Click Here To Continue Reading Daddy's Best Friend

About the Author

Kelli writes billionaires, bad boys, and alpha protectors that are hot-as-sin and filthy to the core. If you want to stay up to date with all things Kelli, sign up to her mailings list here.

Also by Kelli Callahan

Forbidden Kiss

Obsessed With A Daddy

Indebted To A Daddy

Beast Daddy

My Bully's Daddy

Interview With A Daddy

Daddy's Best Friend

Best Friend's Daddy

Distinguished Daddy

Caged By Them

Ravaged By Them

Broken By Them

Ruined By Them

Taken By Them

Surrender To Them Box Set

CPSIA information can be obtained
at www.ICGtesting.com
Printed in the USA
FSHW021942070819
60833FS

9 781086 884258